Murder in the Generative Kitchen

Meg Pontecorvo

World Weaver Press

MURDER IN THE GENERATIVE KITCHEN

Meg Pontecorvo
Copyright © 2016 Meg Schoerke.

This is a work of fiction; characters and events are either fictitious or used
fictitiously.

Published by World Weaver Press, LLC
Albuquerque, NM
www.WorldWeaverPress.com
Editor: Sarena Ulibarri
Cover layout and design by Sarena Ulibarri.
Cover images used under license from Shutterstock.com.

First edition: September 2016
ISBN-13: 978-0-9977888-1-5

Also available as an ebook

Murder in the Generative Kitchen

Picking lint from her rumpled blue cardigan, McConnery Ellis, the only human in the virtual courtroom, slumped at the defense table beside her cylindrical steel attorney. Like the other robotic sims surrounding her—gray judge, blue prosecutor, purple jurors—the spring-green defense bot was a cheap model, with an expressionless face and a body whose range of motion varied according to which attorney manipulated it in the control room. Its polished torso, buffed to a liquid sheen, reflected the courtroom like a funhouse mirror.

At a nod from the judge, the blue prosecution bot rose for the opening statement. It bowed to the judge and faced the video camera affixed to the right corner of the jury box.

"Members of the jury," said the blue bot, "the woman sitting in front of you is a killer. On the night of September tenth, 2060, the defendant, McConnery Ellis, prepared dinner for her husband, George Alexander Ellis. They had been married thirty-two years, and they ate together most evenings. At approximately 7:00 p.m., Mrs. Ellis brought his meal to the table and joined him a minute later with hers. Just after she sat down, he took a few bites and collapsed. She called 911. The medics arrived eight minutes later to find him dead.

You will learn from their testimony that scans of his body revealed traces of cyanide, which was later confirmed by police pathologists as the immediate cause of death. After the team failed to resuscitate Mr. Ellis, the head medic scanned his meal—trout almondine, served with almond garnished rice and green beans—and found cyanide. Mrs. Ellis's food was poison-free.

"Mrs. Ellis had the resource, a generative kitchen, to create a meal infused with cyanide. Moreover, she had a motive. A year before his death, Mr. Ellis had retired from his position as Executive Vice President of Signature Ventures Corporation. But after he transitioned to a life of leisure, Mrs. Ellis had problems adjusting to his constant presence at home. She spent more and more time in the kitchen. On the afternoon of September tenth, the Ellises argued about her use of said kitchen. That evening, she went into the kitchen and prepared George Ellis's final meal. Trout almondine, laced with cyanide.

"On the night of her husband's death, no other person came near that kitchen while Mrs. Ellis made dinner. And the evidence will show that the presence of cyanide in Mr. Ellis's food was no accident: the advanced nature of a generative kitchen leaves no possibility for error. Likewise, because a generative kitchen must be programmed to suit its owner's needs, Mrs. Ellis must have carefully planned the means and method of her husband's demise.

"The evidence is irrefutable. It leads to only one conclusion: McConnery Ellis should be found guilty of murder, in the first degree."

The blue bot bowed to the camera and returned to the prosecution table. McConnery Ellis continued to pick at her sweater. A lank strand of gray hair fell across her forehead, and she tucked it behind her left ear.

The green bot rose, its joints creaking, and lurched to the center of the courtroom.

"Members of the jury," it said in a flat, metallic voice. "Mrs.

McConnery Ellis—Connie, as she is known to friends and family—has just been described to you as a calculating, cold-blooded murderer. But ask yourselves: does she look like a murderer?"

Mrs. Ellis turned to face the fourteen purple juror bots in their tiered benches on the right side of the courtroom. The faceless, genderless bots, not designed for movement, remained riveted to their seats.

The green bot swiveled to the defense table and tapped its acrylic surface. Mrs. Ellis extended her neck and squinted to read the embedded screen. She sighed, smoothed her blouse collar over her cardigan, and reoriented herself to face the camera.

The defense bot paused while the camera focused on her for a close-up. "Sometimes, first impressions don't lie," said the bot. "Connie Ellis is as she appears. A middle-aged housewife, dedicated to her husband. A woman who loves to cook. And a woman who became, unfortunately, a victim of technological circumstance."

The camera pulled back from its close-up, and the bot stepped in front of it. "How, then, was Mr. Ellis poisoned? Yes, Connie Ellis served him that meal. And she sat down at the table to join him for dinner, as she had done almost every night for the duration of their marriage. But she received the shock of her life when he collapsed. For, although she selected the meal, shopped for its ingredients, and participated in its creation, she did not apply the cyanide garnish that killed her husband.

"The evidence will show that this poor woman deserves acquittal. McConnery Ellis is not guilty of murder. Why? Because the perpetrator is, in fact, the kitchen."

🏝

Red lights flashed at the periphery of his vision, and Julio González tore off his headset, leapt from a wicker chair in the lobby, where he had settled to watch the vidstream of the opening statements, and sprinted through the sliding doors to the broad beachfront patio. He ducked into a peppermint-striped cabana just as the sirens began to blare. Somewhere on the premises of the Vacation Jury Resort Hotel, a juror must have spoken, breaking the sequestration oath. Julio wondered if the violator was a newbie, like him.

The sirens died down, and Julio moved to a chaise lounge. He unbuttoned his shirt, stretched his legs on the wooden slats, and wished he had brought a towel from his room. The pool looked inviting, despite being shaped like the state of Illinois.

Clutching their vidstream headsets, people straggled out of the lobby and shaded their eyes. Julio recognized a few of them from the plane the night before: the rheumy-eyed blonde who had sat across the aisle and sneezed non-stop; a big-bellied man wearing a red Hawaiian shirt; a young woman, perhaps a student, with a backpack slung over her shoulder; and an old woman, her face shaded by a floppy brimmed straw hat. Julio considered giving them a friendly nod, then glanced at a surveillance camera poking through the thatch of the tiki bar. Even an inappropriate gesture from a juror could set off the alarms and result in eviction from the hotel.

The rules were strict here. Yet he still couldn't believe his good luck. The odds of being selected to serve in the Vacation Jury Program were worse than cleaning up at the holoslots in one of the Federal casinos along Lake Michigan. But here he was, poolside in the Acapulco hotel owned by the Circuit Court of Cook County, while his simulacrum sat in the jury box in sub-zero Chicago.

He wished he still had his phone. Like all the other jurors, he had surrendered it to court officials at the airport in Chicago as a condition of participating in the program. But now he itched to snap a selfie and send it to Toni, his ex—or, maybe, soon-to-be-ex—girlfriend. The night before he left, they had fought and reached their usual ridiculous stalemate. Toni was such a great match for him in so many ways: she still turned him on after four years together; she shared his absurdist sense of humor, and they scoured the art house film listings in Chicago to find screenings of 20th century screwball comedies; she was a huge basketball fan and cheered just as loudly as he did when they watched Bulls games together in sports bars; she even lived around the block from him on Chicago's North Side. And, as a marathon runner, she had a lean, toned body. So he just couldn't understand why she refused to be more feminine—wear make-up, fashionable clothes, or act flirty with him—especially when they went out. It wasn't much to ask, and it was all their relationship needed to be perfect. But no, whenever he raised the topic—even gently—she became cold and sarcastic and suggested that *he* was the problem— that he needed to get over his machismo and join the 21st century. Then he would fly into a rage, and—

He realized that he was gripping the arms of the chaise lounge. He exhaled slowly, reminding himself that he was here to relax and forget about Toni. They had agreed to use his stint on Vacation Jury Duty as a cooling-off period. Well, a blizzard was predicted for Chicago that week—just the "cool-off" she deserved while he was living the high life in sunny Acapulco.

Thinking about Toni, he wished he had not his own phone, but one of those Sensurround phones, so that he could annoy her with a selfie that captured the gorgeous sights of the resort and the sounds and smells, too. Palm fronds clattered above him, and he closed his eyes to savor the soothing rhythm. Beyond the patio, waves crashed on the shore. Gulls screamed. He smelled salt water, warm sand, the sweet aroma of coconut tanning oil, and—tomatoes?

He opened his eyes. The woman beside him was sipping a Virgin Mary. He thought about ordering one from the tiki bar. Unlike meals, drinks here weren't on the house—even the virgin ones served to people who hadn't finished watching their trial footage for the day. No, he decided to wait. He had a limited budget for extras like drinks and room service, and he had no idea how long "The People versus McConnery Ellis" would last. The sooner he got through the seven hour testimony stream, the sooner he could order a real drink. He was required to finish viewing the day's footage by midnight, and he wasn't the kind of man to procrastinate. At least, he could never afford to procrastinate back home in his job as Deputy Assistant Sub-regional Coordinator at Allied Packaging Insurance, Inc. He was happy to take a break from the phone and its constant alerts about bubble wrap recalls and delivery drone drops gone astray.

He leaned back against the deckchair and strapped on the headgear. Damn. In his rush to escape the lobby, he forgot to pause the vidstream. The opening statements were done. With the sun caressing his skin, he felt too lazy to replay them. Oh, well. He decided that being a Vacation Juror wasn't quite like his job in Chicago, where every problem had to be instantly solved. He could review both opening statements later, after a swim.

Julio adjusted the headset until its cushioned forehead piece conformed to his temples. He smoothed down the mesh side flaps to cut the glare.

A redheaded woman was testifying. Julio flicked the control pod, and her credentials scrolled across the screen: Melissa Zymboski, EMT. As she described the team's arrival and unsuccessful efforts to resuscitate Mr. Ellis, the camera lingered on Mrs. Ellis. The close-up magnified every wrinkle, as well as her salt-and-pepper hair, the hollows under her eyes, and her double chin. Of course, the court prohibited defendants from preparing for the trial by doctoring their appearances through body sculpting. But Mrs. Ellis looked so frumpish that he doubted she had ever set foot in a sculpting studio—which seemed odd for the wife of a wealthy businessman.

Julio fiddled with the controls to see if he could switch the camera angle or viewpoint. No luck. He increased his thumb pressure on the touch pad and the contrast changed. The bluescreen behind Mrs. Ellis faded, replaced by shadowy images of the patio: palm trunks, umbrellaed tables, the tiki bar. Now he understood how jurors could wander around the resort while wearing their headsets. He craned his neck, rearranging his field of vision to position Mrs. Ellis beside the tiki bar. He turned his head. Even better: a parade of shadow people sauntered across the patio on their way to the beach cabanas.

Bored by the testimony, he began to track the silhouettes of bikini-clad women, following one, then switching in favor of a better specimen, until, over Mrs. Ellis's left shoulder, a rainbow danced along the opposite edge of the pool.

He felt as if he were staring through a kaleidoscope. As the silhouette moved, the colors scrambled: cobalt and magenta, gold and mother-of-pearl, flickering along perfectly proportioned female curves—so different from Toni's lean, boyish body.

He took off the headset to behold the vision. Balancing one foot on a deckchair, a petite young woman wound her long bronze braid into a loose knot at the nape of her neck. She was shorter than Toni, who was exactly his height.

He guessed that this woman was in her early twenties. She wore a white bandeau, which barely covered her generous breasts, and a tiny ruffled swim skirt. Along the rich brown skin of her arms and legs ran swirls of iridescence. Julio had heard about the process—a biometallic lacquer applied to the skin—but had never known anyone who had dared to try it. The polarization on his headset must have magnified the effect.

Catching the sunlight, the colors swirled across the darkness of her skin. *Iris*, he thought. *Arco iris. Rainbow girl.*

She stripped off her sandals and dipped a toe in the water. Julio stood, took a step in her direction, and paused as he remembered the sequestration rules. He glanced at the surveillance camera and sat down again on the edge of a chaise lounge.

She stretched her arms skyward, bent, and dove, leaving a shimmer of bubbles in her wake. Julio held his breath and waited for her to surface. She swam two laps, dodging people wading in the shallow end, and climbed out. The wet swimsuit clung to her body, and Julio tightened his grip on the chair slats. She shook the braid out of its knot, scooped up her sandals, and draped a plush towel over her shoulders.

As she pranced up the steps to the lobby, Julio noticed a surveillance camera poised above the sliding glass doors. He wondered if the security team had enjoyed the show as much as he did.

The prosecution opened the second day of testimony with a recording of the emergency call. A distraught Mrs. Ellis veered into view on the screen, her face too close to the camera. Her cheeks were flushed, and her pupils were dilated.

"Help. Please. George—my husband. He's collapsed."

She glanced over her shoulder and then moved to the side of the screen. Blurred in the background, a man slumped over the dining room table.

"Is he still breathing?" asked the dispatcher.

"Yes. I mean, no. Not now. I tried to give him the Heimlich, I—" Mrs. Ellis burst into tears. "*Just come.*"

"Hang on," said the dispatcher. "A team is on its way."

The recording dissolved, and the camera zoomed in on Mrs. Ellis sitting at the defense table, hands clutched in her lap.

Testifying first was the toxicological pathologist, Emery Bixby, Ph.D., a small man sporting thick black glasses. He certified that George Ellis had died from acute cyanide poisoning. Prompted by the prosecutor, he detailed the pain and suffering that Mr. Ellis likely experienced as the cyanide raced through his system.

". . . And did your lab discover the source of the cyanide?" asked the blue bot.

"Yes. After testing samples of the meal, we determined that almonds in the garnish were saturated with cyanide: a lethal dose."

"And where could Mrs. Ellis could have obtained the poison?" asked the blue bot.

"Objection," countered the green bot. "The question presupposes Mrs. Ellis as the murderer."

"Sustained," said the gray judge bot. "The prosecution will

rephrase the question."

"Of course," said the blue bot. "Dr. Bixby, did you identify the source of the cyanide?"

Dr. Bixby adjusted his glasses. "According to the kitchen's logs, the cyanide was synthesized on the premises, at 6:55 p.m., from the almonds themselves. The trace cyanide in the almond skins was hyped-up—bioengineered—to a potency 500% higher than normal, enough to kill Mr. Ellis after only a few bites."

The blue bot turned to face the jurycam. "But Mrs. Ellis is a housewife, with a college degree in English. Would she have had the knowledge to increase the potency of the cyanide in the almonds she served her husband?"

"I can't speculate about her capabilities," the toxicologist replied, "but information about the poison content of bitter almonds is widely available, and her kitchen could easily perform such a task. Its design parameters enable it to alter the biochemistry of the food it processes."

On cross-examination, the defense bot asked the witness to scrutinize the autopsy report, which the prosecution had made available on the vidscreens as an exhibit.

"Dr. Bixby, for the record, can you please explain the findings you describe in the autopsy's third paragraph?"

Dr. Bixby peered at the screen embedded in the broad railing of the witness box. "Certainly. The body exhibited advanced adenocarcinoma of the pancreas, with extensive metastatic involvement of the liver."

"Can you simplify that assessment?"

"Mr. Ellis suffered from terminal pancreatic cancer."

"Terminal? Was the cancer advanced enough to have caused his death?"

"As I have already testified, the immediate cause of death was ingestion of hydrogen cyanide. The carcinoma's metastasis would likely have caused liver failure eventually."

"Was Mr. Ellis taking any anti-cancer drugs?"

"The tissue analysis summary in paragraph four shows that Mr. Ellis had been taking a subdermal synthetic tropane alkaloid—a palliative, for pain management of terminal cancer."

"Would that have blunted any of the pain and suffering normally experienced by a victim of cyanide poisoning?"

Dr. Bixby hesitated. "Possibly. But we have no way of knowing. Research into poison palliation has never been pursued, at least in this country."

"Has such research been done elsewhere? By hospice scientists in Europe, for example, where euthanasia is legal and commonly practiced?"

The blue bot rapped on its table. "Objection. Dr. Bixby is not a medical researcher."

"Sustained," said the judge bot. "The defense will limit its questions to those appropriate to the witness's expertise."

The green bot switched off the display screen. "Dr. Bixby, can you clarify your assertion that knowledge about the almond-derived cyanide is 'widely available'?"

"I meant that, on a home or mobile vidscreeen, anyone can enter 'cyanide' as a search term and discover bitter almonds as a source."

"Is that all? Are there sites that reveal how to bioengineer almonds to create enough cyanide to kill a person?"

"Yes."

"And, in your professional opinion, could someone with no lab expertise whatsoever, follow the instructions given on such sites?"

The toxicologist hesitated again. "I don't see why not. Even for a layman, it would be like following a recipe."

"Oh really?" snapped the defense bot. "Bioengineering in ten easy steps?"

Dr. Bixby shook his head. "It's not a matter of the person's expertise. With the database presets and option for accelerant net enhancement, the hyper-functionality, and the user-to-content adapto-buffering capabilities of a generative kitchen, anyone could perform bio-engineering tasks related to food."

"Can you restate your point in less technical language?"

"I mean that these kitchens—they're like having a home laboratory. And their job is to simplify food-related tasks. The *kitchen* can do all the work."

"So the kitchen could have bioengineered the cyanide without any participation from the defendant?"

"Well, yes, but someone would have to initiate the process —give the command."

"How explicit would that command need to be?" asked the defense bot.

"Objection," said the prosecution bot. "Dr. Bixby is not an expert on state-of-the-art kitchens."

"Overruled," replied the judge bot and nodded at the witness.

"I'm sorry," said Dr. Bixby. "Would you repeat the question?"

"Can a generative kitchen alter food to bioengineer poison, with no direct command from a human being?"

"As I understand the technology, we would need to reinterpret the concept of 'command,' since generative kitchens are intended to assess and respond to the desires of their owners, conscious or unconscious. But I don't think that such a kitchen could act on its own volition. A generative kitchen is a machine, and there are fail-safes."

The defense bot leaned forward and gripped the railing of the witness box. "But Mr. Ellis is dead, sir. And, according to the kitchen's own logs, the cyanide was processed as a component of the meal, in the kitchen and by the kitchen, on the night the meal was served. So, I ask you again: based on your understanding of the bioengineering of cyanide from bitter almonds, would a generative kitchen be able to make the poison—or, really, make the almonds excessively poisonous—on its own agency?"

"No, I don't think so. I can't imagine how the protocols against that could go wrong."

After dinner on the third day, Julio lounged on one of the lobby's broad rattan couches, flicking through the trial's exhibit photos on the headset while hoping to spot Iris. After her spectacular debut at the pool yesterday, she seemed to have disappeared. Julio hadn't crossed paths with her on the patio, or at meals, or during what he had decided to call the pantomime happy hour, due to its silence, and the patrons ignoring one another, at the tiki bar. He mentally kicked himself to think that she may have left already, likely with a planeload of jurors bound for deliberation in Chicago.

He skipped through technical stuff like the autopsy report to the photos that the prosecution had posted during the testimony of two police detectives. The blue bot had repeatedly called the dining room "the scene of the crime." Apart from the fact that the Ellises were wealthy enough to have a dining room, the place looked unremarkable—not like the blood-spattered rooms Julio had seen on reality crime shows.

Nor was the victim as gruesome as Julio would have expected. George Ellis lay supine on the blue oriental carpet, surrounded by resuscitation equipment. In the headshot, his bloodshot eyes had rolled slightly upward, his skin was bright pink, and his jowls sagged like a punctured balloon. Flecks of rice stuck to his chin.

Julio fast-forwarded to gape at the kitchen, where everything was restaurant grade. Even the auto-cook modules were larger than the tiny units wedged into the kitchen nooks of micro-apartments like his own. The retro design included a six burner titanium stove, ample cabinets, gleaming countertops, and a real wood chopping block— things that hadn't been standard in kitchen design for over twenty years.

As he scrolled through the photos, Julio thought back to the few times a year that his mother had cooked during his childhood: only on holidays, and the meals were never as tasty as the ones fixed by the auto-prep machine. Those dinners seemed interminable, since his mother's timing was always off, with gaps of twenty or thirty minutes between servings of lumpy mashed potatoes, dry meat, oversteamed vegetables, and, for dessert, underbaked pie. By the time he was ten, his mother finally conceded to the family's reassurances that she could show her love for them just as well through auto-prepping pizzas for Thanksgiving and Christmas. When he was in his teens, they upgraded to an apartment that had no kitchen at all: just an auto-module wedged in a hallway closet, with the real apparatus—the dish formatter and crusher, and the storage, prep, and cook machines—tucked behind the wall.

When he could finally afford to move into his own micro-apartment, part of what made him feel like an adult was the tiny auto-cook module, complete with the latest food printing technology, installed in a small cabinet beside the bathroom. No one in his building even shopped for food anymore; the fees for keeping the nutrient pastes streaming to the printer and auto-cooker were included in the rent. If he wanted fancier food, he ate out.

Lingering over a wide-angle photo of the Ellis kitchen, he marveled at the scale. Not counting the enormous pantry, the kitchen was almost the size of his apartment. Julio snorted. With the advent of the sixty-hour work week, no one had time to cook anymore, except the rich.

Or the luxury to murder a spouse through bioengineering cyanide? Julio wondered. He had a hard time thinking of the defendant as a murderess. She seemed so ordinary, like somebody's mother, although she and her husband were childless. Generative kitchens weren't cheap, so he doubted that her motive was money. Could passion grip someone so bland? Maybe she had a lover. Or maybe she wanted to spare her husband a protracted death from cancer.

Julio pressed the magnification button and scrutinized the layout. In the space between the dish-crusher and bioreactive composter darted an iridescent gleam, like a hummingbird. Adjusting the backscreen contrast, he saw Iris stepping through the lobby's sliding doors. He switched off the headset, tucked it into its carrying case, and followed her to the patio.

Passing tables where a few lone jurors sipped drinks, she headed through the wrought-iron gate to the beach. Julio closed the sliding doors and paused beside the pool. The gentle luau music playing over the speakers alongside the tiki bar made him wince. He would have expected a resort in Acapulco to feature Mex-pop, which he loved. He hurried through the patio area, as much to escape the soundtrack as to follow Iris.

The beach fronting the hotel was partitioned from other resort properties on the strip with a festive barbed-wire fence strung with chili pepper Christmas lights. The area was much less crowded now than it was during the day. Watching the sunset through their headsets, a few people sat in the cabanas or leaned against the palms near the patio wall. Beyond the rows of identical chaise lounges that extended along half the resort's beach, Iris was the only person who strolled along the water line.

Julio kicked off his sandals, unbuttoned his shirt, and sauntered through the gate, enjoying how cool the sand felt between his toes. He threw back his shoulders and smiled as the warm breeze tickled his chest. Then he set off after Iris, his pace casual. There was no chance she could out-walk him. The barbed wire fence limited her range.

Before she reached the barrier, Iris waded knee deep in the surf, her gauzy beach wrap and unbraided hair rippling in the breeze. Julio was struck by how different she looked than Toni—who, he knew, would have taken a sunset run on the beach, like she did on summer nights along Lake Michigan. She would come back tired and sweaty, her short hair plastered so smoothly to her head by her runner's headband that she would look almost bald.

He raised a hand to his forehead as a shield against the sun, and to admire Iris's curvy silhouette. Of course, he respected Toni's athletic grace. But Iris was the girl for him.

As the sun disappeared beneath the wall of the huge dike protecting Acapulco Bay, the western sky's reds shifted to purples. Julio positioned himself diagonally behind Iris, just above the tideline. Rising in the east behind the hotel, the full moon glinted off her biometallic lacquer and outlined her body in wavering colors.

A wave set rolled in, and water surged against her thighs. She wheeled, flashed him a smile, then turned away, intent on the skyscape.

He tried to think of an appropriate opener, but his brain only stuttered out clichÃ©s. No—he'd keep it simple, say "Hello, beautiful evening," and gaze at her meaningfully enough to show that he complimented more than the scenery. But as he stepped into the water, he felt a hand tighten around his forearm.

"Good evening, sir." A mustachioed security guard in a khaki uniform drew him back. Iris turned again, and the guard motioned her to approach. She positioned herself beside Julio, close enough that her loose hair brushed against his right shoulder. His heart fluttered.

"Since you're both recent arrivals, here's a friendly reminder," said the guard. "You're welcome to enjoy the amenities, but you must not communicate with your fellow jurors

—by any means. Violation of the sequestration rules will result in expulsion from the resort, and, since you will no longer be able to fulfill your civic duty, the Circuit Court of Cook County would have to charge you for your resort stay and the round trip flight. Understand?"

"No problem, sir. I was just enjoying the view." Julio winked.

The guard remained impassive. "Mr. González, only *one* of you should remain here on the beach."

Iris stepped away from Julio, smiled wistfully at the moon, and sashayed back into the surf.

Julio turned and walked back to the hotel, dragging his feet in the sand.

On the fourth day, the prosecutor called a close friend of the defendant to the stand. Like Mrs. Ellis, Geraldine Parker was in her mid-fifties, but she looked thirty years younger. Blonde and buxom, she accentuated her bodywork with a scoop-necked velvet jacket, a tight skirt, and thigh high snakeskin boots. Her flawless face lacked the rigidity characteristic of low-end body sculptors: she could afford the best in the business.

The prosecutor approached the stand. "Kindly tell the jury: How long have you known McConnery Ellis?"

"Around thirty-six years," said Mrs. Parker in a breathy voice. "We were sorority sisters—Tri Delts—at Northwestern."

"When did Mrs. Ellis install her generative kitchen?"

"About two years ago. When George retired from Signature Ventures Corporation, he cashed in on his stock options and gave Connie a choice: either have the works—the age-defying body and facial treatment—done at Michelangelo's on Michigan Avenue, or get her dream kitchen."

"And she chose the kitchen?"

"Yes."

"Did you, as her close friend, advise her to made that choice?"

Mrs. Parker squared her shoulders and shook her blonde ringlets. "Certainly not! We—myself and Connie's other girlfriends—were in fact shocked. I mean, we knew she wanted to cook, but she'd seen what Michelangelo's did for us! Before George retired, he never allowed her to have any refab—said it was too expensive—and whenever one of us came back from the studio, she acted real self-conscious about her looks. We tried to be charitable, but we didn't invite her shopping anymore. Trying on clothes together was impossible, since the rest of us buy from the teen department!" She tucked her hair behind her ears and resettled herself on the edge of her chair, displaying Michelangelo's handiwork from a new angle.

"Why do you think she wanted the kitchen, instead of the bodywork?"

The witness gave a conspiratorial wink at Mrs. Ellis, who ignored her. "We all thought it was to spite George."

The defense bot rose. "Objection—this is mere speculation, your honor."

"Sustained. The prosecution will rephrase the question."

The blue bot nodded curtly. "Did Mrs. Ellis tell you why she chose the kitchen?"

"Well, she was angry at George for making her have to choose. She said that, with the money he got from SigVent, she should have had both, but he was such a penny pincher that he wanted to reinvest most of it."

"How often did Mrs. Ellis use the kitchen?"

"Every day. Cooking was her passion—and George, he loved to eat. He himself patronized Michelangelo's for the occasional nip and tuck, if you know what I mean! But Connie never knew—that is, until I told her."

"How and when did you find out about his visits to Michelangelo's?"

"I saw him in one of the quick-sculpt booths, about six months before he died."

"And when did you tell Mrs. Ellis?"

"As soon as I could. I called her on my way home."

"And what was her reaction?"

"She was furious."

The prosecution bot paused. Mrs. Parker recrossed her legs and smoothed her skirt.

"Did Mrs. Ellis confide in you about her relationship with her husband?" the blue bot continued. "Did he treat her well?"

"Before he left SigVent, she didn't complain much, except about his tight hand on the purse strings. They got along okay
—at least, I never noticed any problems. But after he retired, well,

he was around the house constantly, and that drove her crazy! She said she kept nagging him to find a hobby or do charity work or *something*. But she said that he said that he deserved a leisurely retirement, and—"

The defense bot sprang up. "Objection: Hearsay."

"Sustained," said the judge bot.

The prosecution bot began again. "Did you witness any disputes between Mr. and Mrs. Ellis?"

"Yes. After he retired, she spent more and more time in the kitchen. At least, that's what she told me. And I—we all

—could tell, because she invited us over for some amazing luncheons!"

"How often did she hold these luncheons?"

"Every Friday."

"Did Mr. Ellis join you?"

"No, sir. The luncheons were for us girls. I think she got lonely when we quit shopping with her, so she started the Friday lunch thing. Her kitchen was the International Model, so she served a new cuisine every week. By the time George passed, we'd eaten our way around half the Mediterranean!"

"Was Mr. Ellis home during the luncheons?"

"Usually. We didn't always see him, but Connie would joke about trying to get him out of the house. Sometimes he'd make an appearance, and she'd shoo him off."

"Did he comply?"

"If he'd eaten already—Connie served him the same lunch as us, but made him eat alone—he'd give his compliments to the chef and disappear. But there was one time—whoo, boy, they really went at it!"

"They argued?"

"Yes."

"Can you describe the argument? What did it concern?"

"It was awful. It was right after lunch, and he'd been out

somewhere. He came in asking to be fed and exploded when she said she'd only prepared enough for us girls. He accused her of paying more attention to the kitchen than to him. She accused him of being a hypocrite for going to Michelangelo's. He said he'd have the kitchen (he called it 'the damned kitchen') torn out. She said he shouldn't have retired unless he'd figured out what else to do. Then he said that there was no point in doing anything anymore and blamed her for making his life miserable. They went round and round."

"Did you hear how the argument concluded?"

"No. We all left as fast as we could—politely, of course."

"And when did this argument take place?"

Mrs. Parker raised her knuckle to her lips. "The day he died."

That evening, Julio sat in the cafeteria after dinner, sipping an espresso and calculating. The guard last night had called them both "recent arrivals," so Julio suspected that Iris was on his jury. If she found him attractive, then maybe she would stroll on the beach at the same time as last night, so that they could connect. But if he followed her, the guards might notice—or, worse, Iris might think he was stalking her. No, he would have to be discreet. Better to whet her appetite. Make her come to him.

To gauge the time, he turned toward the picture window on the west side of the cafeteria. The sun hung just above the dike horizon. Leaving his espresso half-finished, Julio leapt up so fast that he knocked his chair backwards onto the floor. The noise shattered the cafeteria's usual, low-level soundscape of utensils scraping against plates and the whoosh of ice and soda from the beverage machines. Jurors all over the room turned to look at him and then quickly glanced down at their food or out the window. Julio was grateful that the sequestration rules prevented people from singling him out with long, punishing stares. As he made his way to the door, he thought about mouthing "sorry" to the few jurors who still shot glances at him, but he decided he had drawn enough attention to himself for one evening.

Yet there was one person's attention he was determined to gain. He saw the beach guard's warning as a challenge, rather than a prohibition. A feminine woman like Iris would naturally be impressed by a man bold enough to beat the system. Getting her attention would be only the first step.

Avoiding the sluggish elevator, he sprinted up the emergency stairs to his room on the second floor. On the day he arrived, he was annoyed to have been assigned a room overlooking the pool. Now, he thanked the gods—Christian, Aztec, and Tiki gods, too.

He turned off all the lights, slid open the balcony's glass door, and stood in the darkness, watching.

Five minutes later, Iris sauntered barefoot across the patio, her long hair and gauzy beach dress billowing behind her.

When she stepped through the gate and disappeared from view, Julio flipped on the lights, stripped to the waist, and stationed himself in the center of the balcony.

Unable to see the shore over the patio wall and palm fronds, he leaned against the railing and waited, feeling alternately exhilarated that Iris might notice him when she returned and terrified that she might find his ardor comical.

The longer he waited, the more the gentle luau soundtrack from the tiki bar grated on him. His mind drifted to the trial. He thought about replaying the testimony to drown out the music, but the headgear looked stupid, and he wanted to make the right impression on Iris.

So he continued his vigil. Twenty minutes passed. The sky darkened to indigo. A few people straggled in from the beach, but not Iris. What was she doing? He fantasized about sending off a drone to spy on her, and about how she would look from an aerial perspective, but thinking about drones reminded him of processing insurance claims for delinquent packages. He shifted his focus back to Iris and imagined her stripping off the blowsy beach wrap and diving into the waves, and how she would rise naked from the surf like in that painting by—what was his name? Vermicelli?—except Iris wouldn't need a half shell because her iridescent skin would shimmer in the lingering light like a warm brown pearl.

Hearing the gate clang, he shook himself out of his reverie. Iris stepped onto the patio, then paused to brace one hand against a palm trunk and brush the sand from her lovely feet. In the reddish glow of the tiki bar's faux torches, her hair seemed orange rather than bronze, and fell across her shoulders in long waves.

Julio thought again of that painting. Should he call her Venus? No—*Iris* was better. Granting him only fleeting glimpses, she was as transitory as a rainbow. Well, before she disappeared again, he would give her a sight to admire.

He inhaled and threw back his shoulders so that she could appraise his body, outlined against the illuminated white curtain that stirred in the ceiling fan's breeze.

She glanced up and just as swiftly leveled her head as she passed a surveillance camera. Crossing the patio, she maintained such a steady posture that Julio knew she was watching him.

On cross-examination, the defense bot inquired whether Mrs. Parker knew that Mr. Ellis suffered from cancer. She was surprised and claimed that Mrs. Ellis couldn't have known about his condition, since she would have certainly told all her friends. After asking a few questions that implied the friendship was superficial, the defense bot changed tactics.

"Mrs. Parker, when you were at the Ellis's house, did you spend time in the kitchen?"

"Oh yes. Connie always served us drinks there before lunch, so she could show it off. I mean, to have a kitchen that responds to you— takes your biometrics before every meal and adjusts everything as it learns more about you—that's amazing!"

"Did Mrs. Ellis give you the chance to experience this aspect of the kitchen?"

"Yes—with the coffee. Connie let us fix our own, using the Robo-Barrista mode, and the kitchen recorded our preferences. The next week, it served us the same."

"Exactly the same?"

"Well, not exactly. Each week the caffeine level would be different, depending on our bioreadings. Once, I'd drunk too much champagne the night before, and the kitchen served me a triple espresso: just what I needed!"

"Did she explain the kitchen's ability to adjust not only drinks, but food servings, based on biometrics?"

"Oh, she bragged about that all the time—said the kitchen was making her and George extra healthy by adding vitamins and stuff to their food."

"Did that happen with your meals at the luncheons?"

"Connie said no—the kitchen didn't have enough data on us. Apparently, the kitchen develops a relationship with its users."

"What kind of relationship?"

"It makes decisions, based on their desires and needs. Connie said that every day it got better at knowing what she wanted—to eat, that is."

"And how much time did she spend in the kitchen?"

"Hours. She joked that she only went out to shop for ingredients! The kitchen was teaching her all sorts of cooking styles."

"How did the process work?"

"For methods she had mastered, it would play sous-chef, and she would take control. But on other days, like when she was learning a new technique or chatting with us before lunch, she would chop or stir or sautÃ© as it directed."

"And how did the kitchen communicate with her?"

Mrs. Parker smirked. "The instructional voices she chose were always the sexy ones. The male voices, with accents—French, Italian,

Spanish—all keyed to whatever kind of cooking she was learning. No wonder George was jealous!"

Julio did his best to keep up the pretense of a weekend, despite having to watch testimony. Politics exacted a double-standard: to recruit jurors for long trials, the taxpayers were willing to fund the vacation jury system; but they didn't tolerate jurors taking a vacation, so there were no days off or weekend breaks. Julio treated himself to breakfast in bed on Saturday and slogged through the testimony of Mrs. Ellis's three other regular luncheon guests. Their cattiness made him feel sorry for Mrs. Ellis, but he also wondered what sort of person she was to have such shallow friends.

After dinner, he positioned himself on the balcony and angled himself in the pose of a Greek statue he had seen in the Art Institute. Iris rewarded him by diving into the pool and swimming two laps of breaststroke, her head poised above the water as if she were balancing a martini glass.

On Sunday, he snagged a poolside Adirondack chair and faced it toward the sun, away from the nearest surveillance cameras. He purchased a Virgin Mary and nursed it as he assessed the prosecution's final witnesses: two body techs from Michelangelo's, who substantiated that Mr. Ellis frequented the studio during the year before his death.

Idly, Julio unspeared a pickled onion from the swizzle stick and began doodling in tomato juice on the cocktail napkin. He dipped the stick in the drink, doodled some more on the back of a coaster, and set it to dry in the sun while he dozed through the second tech's testimony.

An alarm woke him. Another sequestration breach somewhere in the hotel. Through half-closed eyes, he watched a few frightened jurors leap from their chaises, tear off their headsets, and look around questioningly. Julio yawned and stretched his arms. He already felt like an old-timer. Only newbies were startled by the alarms.

The vidstream had run its course, and his skin ached from sun exposure. He sat up straight in his chair, removed his headset, and glanced at the coaster. There was his room number, 257, pale red, but legible.

That night, after Iris made her way to the beach, he kept the room lights off as he knelt and leaned the coaster diagonally between the bars of the balcony railing. After fifteen minutes, he hit the light switch and lounged on the balcony.

Iris returned to the patio a few minutes later. As she passed beneath his room, he turned his back to the railing and nudged the coaster with his foot. Through the acrylic floor of the balcony, he watched the coaster glide downward and fall at Iris's feet. Perfect! She stooped—long enough to read the number—and disappeared into the lobby.

Julio retreated into the room and began to pace. Was she on her way? He checked the room's clock. Would she take the elevator, or the stairs? He returned to the light switch and fiddled with the illumination levels. Had she gone to her room first, to slip into something more comfortable? He imagined her skin, salty after the beach walk, and hoped she hadn't decided to shower.

Julio checked the time again and wiped his palms on his shorts. Eight minutes. Had she seen the room number? Maybe the coaster had fallen wrong-side up.

He heard movement in the hallway, a gentle knock. He exhaled. Just the timbre he would expect from a rainbow girl.

He threw open the door, and a female guard strode in, a plastic club strapped to her belt. A second guard, a man much taller than Julio, lingered in the hall.

The woman reached into her carryall and pulled out the coaster. "We'll consider this strike two, Mr. González," she said. "Our surveillance system is state-of-the-art, including night vision, infrared sensors, and affect recognition technology. Don't try anything else."

Julio yawned, trying to ignore the knot in his stomach. "If your technology is so superior, then you know I'm exhausted and ready for bed."

The guard narrowed her eyes. "We're not kidding, Mr. González. The technology enables us not only to track you, but to anticipate your actions." She tossed the coaster on the bed and strode back into the hallway. "Don't even think of violating your sequestration oath."

"I wouldn't dare," mumbled Julio and shut the door firmly. He shoved the coaster into the trash chute and turned off the lights.

On the ninth day of the trial, the defense called its first witness: T. J. Summers, a marketing vice president for Gen-K, the company behind Mrs. Ellis's kitchen. The VP was even more egregiously sculpted than the techs from Michelangelo's, with a meaty, dimpled chin, rugged cheekbones framing his lavender eyes, and teeth as shiny as white bathroom tiles.

"Mr. Summers," said the defense bot, "please tell the jury: how is a generative kitchen different from an auto-prep module?"

Summers smiled at the jurycam. "The Gen-K is state of the art: the future of health and cooking too!"

"Can you define 'generative'?"

"Glad to. Sometimes, consumers think it means 'generic,' but the name of the game is *to 'generate'*: to create by a natural process, to evolve, to originate, to engender, to procreate, or, when applied to our product, to co-create! And that translates into a kitchen that works with you and evolves according to your habits and desires."

"Was this function of 'co-creation' a main component of the Gen-K 3000, the model installed in the Ellis home?"

"The Gen-K 3000 is top of the line, ahead of its time! The kitchen of the future that grows its databases according to your food preferences, your cooking style, and even your biometrics!"

"Can you explain how this process works? How, for example, would the Gen-K 3000 prepare eggs?"

"Any way you like 'em," grinned the witness, flashing his teeth at the jurycam.

"Okay, but how would 'co-creation' apply?"

"Let's say you like your eggs over-easy. The kitchen can fry 'em up to perfection, using its auto-prep function, but it would also suggest alternatives based on your preference. If you love 'em poached, it may propose runny yolked eggs with hollandaise!"

"But how is this state of the art? Predictions based on consumer selection habits have been part of our culture for almost a century."

"The Gen-K takes that technology to new heights! Over time, through biometric readings and emotion-oriented computing, it does more than make suggestions. Improving with daily use, it makes the *right* suggestions, with an accuracy rate of 98%."

"Accurate in what way?"

"Accurately attuned to *your* body's cravings and biological needs. After doing the biometrics, the Gen-K can tell if you want eggs or cereal, coffee or tea, apple juice or orange juice. And the Gen-K will chemically adjust the food to suit your health needs. So, if you have a history of high cholesterol, the Gen-K will give you a cholesterol-free version of those soft-cooked eggs—and the hollandaise, too!"

"But sir, don't people desire what's *not* good for them? My daughter would prefer ice cream for dinner every night, but my husband and I would never agree to that!"

Summers nodded sagely. "Of course. And the Gen-K is quite capable of synthesizing a bowl of ice cream that would provide your daughter with a nutritionally complete meal!" He leaned back and stretched out his legs. "Customers often indulge themselves when they first install a Gen-K: chocolate cake for breakfast, gingerbread for lunch, crème brulee for dinner, you name it! But, as they work with the kitchen, people recognize how it understands their needs. Accepting the Gen-K's suggestions, they feel deeply satisfied with their meals, physically, mentally, and emotionally, because the food is precisely tailored for them. It's the kind of pleasure that a man with scurvy would feel when eating an orange."

The defense bot cocked its head. "Okay, so the Gen-K can detect vitamin deficiencies and other physiological needs, but how can it *know* that I'd prefer apple juice to orange juice? Or wouldn't it suggest that the man with scurvy should have broccoli, a richer source of vitamin C, instead of an orange? But what if he hates broccoli?"

"That's where the generative aspect comes into play. Over time, as it accumulates data, the Gen-K comes to know such things—that broccoli isn't an option. Moreover, the Gen-K can boost the orange's vitamin C to be the same as in the broccoli." He beamed. "As for knowing whether you'd prefer apple juice to orange juice, desire is, ultimately, a product of biochemistry, and the Gen-K models desire through the most sophisticated data-sensing apparatus available today: not only the biometrics taken from retinal and finger scans, but affect recognition derived from facial expression, posture, tone of voice." He broadened his grin. "The Gen-K knows you better than you know yourself!"

"How does this knowledge apply to cooking?"

"The Gen-K offers food preparation settings that range from the standard, auto-prep mode to what we call 'retro-cook': nearly complete surrender of control to the human operator."

"Nearly complete?" prompted the bot.

"If the human operator—the chef—chooses to make the whole meal with the retro features—stove, oven, and cooking tools galore—the Gen-K will provide the recipe, enhanced ingredients, and act as sous-chef."

"Does 'the operator' only include the person who selects and prepares the meals?"

"The owners of the kitchen determine whom it tracks—usually the family members who consume the meals."

"So, the kitchen would have data on Mr. Ellis, as well as on his wife, and would provide meals for him based on the daily biometrics?"

"That's right."

"How would meals be individualized, when cooked by a human chef? Wouldn't such targeting be difficult if the chef prepared something like spaghetti sauce, which would be divided among family members?"

"The Gen-K has ways of compensating when a chef wants to enjoy the retro-cooking mode and cancel the auto settings."

"Can you be specific?"

"It's simple: the chef will pass each individual's plate through the auto-prep port just before serving, so that the Gen-K can apply a personalized garnish—like a dusting of enhanced parmesan—that would conform the meal to each individual's targeted health needs."

The defense bot asked the witness to examine logs from the Gen-K that the prosecution had introduced into evidence the previous week. "Can you tell us if that was what happened on the evening of Mr. Ellis's death?"

Mr. Summers examined the logs displayed on the witness box screen, furrowed his tanned brow, and frowned.

"Well, sir?" prompted the defense bot.

"According to the logs, Mrs. Ellis assembled the meal herself, and then passed each plate through the auto-port just before serving."

The defense bot stepped closer to the witness stand. "Would the Gen-K have known that Mr. Ellis had metastatic pancreatic cancer?"

"Of course: that would have been clear from the biometrics."

"And how would the Gen-K respond to such a diagnosis?"

Summers leaned back and puffed out his chest. "The Gen-K would plan meals containing cancer-fighting foods: anti-oxidant fruits and vegetables, fresh juices, green tea, beans, certain types of mushrooms. And, of course, it would boost the anti-cancer components on the molecular level." He folded his arms tightly across his chest. "The Gen-K 3000—a perfect choice for the health-conscious consumer with a discriminating palate—is programmed for optimal performance, and adjusts its biometric assessments daily, in tune with your best interests!"

The defense bot faced the jurycam. "But what if a client's illness were terminal? Cures have been found for many kinds of cancer, but pancreatic cancer kills. In fact, many people in Mr. Ellis's condition and income bracket choose to take the 'terminal grand tour' of Europe, where euthanasia is a legal, comfortable, and dignified choice. So, Mr. Summers, would the Gen-K determine that the 'best interest' of Mr. Ellis would be to die, before his illness became painful or debilitating?"

Summers reared back, as if stung. "Of course not! The Gen-K would never—" He took a striped handkerchief from his vest pocket and wiped his brow. "The Gen-K would *never* be proactive in the way that you suggest. No, it would never kill someone, especially an owner! There are protocols and fail-safes!"

The defense bot turned again to face the witness. "Where were those protocols and fail-safes on the night of September tenth? If the Gen-K is programmed not to kill people, then why did it increase the cyanide content of the almonds that garnished George Ellis's meal? If—hypothetically—an owner, say, Mr. Ellis, had specifically asked for a dose of cyanide, then shouldn't the Gen-K be configured to deny such requests?"

Summers's smile froze into a rictus. "It's programmed to work within legal parameters at all times!—and it updates its legal databases every day! Every day!"

On the eighth morning of the trial, Julio stared out the rain-fogged window, flopped over, and went back to sleep. He awoke at noon and breakfasted on a bag of stale potato chips. After watching the Summers testimony for two hours, he rolled out of bed and slit the balcony door to get some air. Rain corrugated the surface of the pool.

Still hungry, he thought of the rich *plátanos con crema*, the side of beans and greasy chorizo, and the cup of thick Mexican chocolate he had for breakfast two days ago. He wondered what a Gen-K would do with those kinds of cravings. Would it take all the pleasure out of eating?

Julio wished that he could see the responses of his fellow-jurors to Summers's revelations. He had found the prosecution's evidence convincing, but now the defense bot's persistent questions about fail-safes made him begin to wonder not only about Mrs. Ellis's guilt, but about whether she should even be on trial. Wasn't customer safety the Gen-K Corporation's responsibility?

He lingered, thinking, beside the balcony door. The wind shifted direction, and a sudden gust blew rain into the room, soaking his face and chest. He slammed the door shut and went to the bathroom to dry off. As he grabbed a towel from the rack, he shrugged. Mrs. Ellis *was* on trial. So that point had already been decided by the court. His duty as a juror was to weigh the facts, not second-guess the system.

He decided to watch the rest of the day's testimony in the lobby. He threw on some clothes and noticed that someone had slipped an envelope under the room's door. Could Iris have somehow obtained writing materials? He grabbed the envelope and tore it open to find not a love letter, but an itemized bill equal to three months of his take-home pay. A note was scrawled on the bottom, signed with a smiley face: "One more strike and you're on your way back to Chicago! The court would not hesitate to garnish your wages!"

Game over, he thought. By now, he wanted not only to hook up with Iris—she was the perfect antidote to Toni!—but also to pull one over on the Vacation Jury guards. But he was not willing to risk losing out on the vacation. At Allied Packaging Insurance, Inc., the work culture was so strict that employees who took more than a few days of vacation time were considered slackers. Of course, Allied Packaging could not legally fire him in retaliation for his participation on a Vacation Jury. But he knew he was pushing his luck by agreeing to serve. Like most employers, Allied Packaging suspended his pay during his jury term, but he had figured that the cut would be a small price to pay for the opportunity to relax in

Acapulco. Not counting the weekends, each day at the resort cost him a day's worth of wages.

But he could not imagine having his wages garnished—in addition to the pay he had already lost—after he returned. His salary was already low enough—due to the high cost, his boss said, of replacing the offshore human claims representatives Julio supervised with increasingly sophisticated bots—that he was terrified of asking for a raise, which would be tantamount to volunteering to be laid off.

Iris haunted his dreams, but the cost of seducing her was too steep. He could not afford to pay the resort costs, nor did he want to be kicked off the jury and lose what might be his only chance in his career at taking a vacation. He jammed the bill in his back pocket. Knowing it was there would fortify him against temptation.

He grabbed his headset and took the elevator to the lobby. Finding a seat proved challenging, however, for many other jurors, including a few he recognized as being assigned to the Ellis trial—the heavy man, and the college age girl—had also decided to flee their rooms and perform their civic duty in a dry public location. All of the comfy chairs were occupied, and, on the twelve sofas strategically scattered throughout the room, only the center cushions were free.

Julio felt awkward about plopping down in a middle seat. Although he thought the guard's warning about affect recognition technology was bogus, he had no doubts that security was tracking him on the surveillance cameras. He was determined to maintain the studied distance from other people that was the *de facto* etiquette in the hotel—until he spied Iris on the end of a fern-patterned couch near the carp pool.

Julio maneuvered across the lobby and lingered in front of the pool. He extended his hand as if to feed the carp, and they roiled the water, mouths agape. Then he patted his back pocket. No, he wouldn't look at her.

He turned his head to scope out a seat elsewhere and was overwhelmed by a heady scent—floral and spicy, like gardenia blossoms dusted with powdered chiles—that overpowered the slightly swampy odor of the carp pool. Iris's perfume! Inhaling, he realized that, since the night he followed her to the beach, he had never been this close to her—only a few steps away.

He shifted his gaze to the carp pool and noticed a surveillance camera nestled in a basket of lush bougainvillea that hung, trailing its flowers, above the fountain. Clever. But the guards couldn't fault him for taking one of the few free seats left in the lobby, could they?

He circled the lobby and inwardly smiled when other jurors took the remaining seats, leaving the cushion next to Iris as the only option. On the opposite end of her couch sat an old woman, whom he recognized as having arrived with his jury group. Her enormous straw purse, decorated with bright crepe flowers, lay on the seat cushion between her and Iris.

The old lady hunched forward, intent on watching her headset. Unsure of how to signal that he wanted to sit down, Julio stood in front of her for what seemed like a century-long minute. She gave no sign that she noticed him. Julio glanced at the bougainvillea basket, then reached out, slid the purse toward the lady, and sat down. Startled, she grunted, lifted her headset, and glared at him. Keeping his expression neutral, Julio cradled his headset and fiddled with the strap. The old woman grabbed the purse and wedged it upright between the cushions, so that it formed a barrier. Frowning, she jerked her headset over her eyes, adjusted the volume, and crossed her arms over her thin chest.

Tense, but relieved that no guards had materialized, Julio risked a glance to his left, toward Iris. Drawing her bare feet under her, Iris turned in his direction, but she was so absorbed in the vidstream that she didn't appear to notice him.

Disappointed, he flicked on his headset and understood: on cross-examination, the prosecutor proceeded to demolish T.J. Summers. Early in the trial, Julio thought that the lawyers were compromised because the sims annulled their humanity, but he understood now that the bot body could be useful to intimidate a witness. The prosecutor worked the sim expertly, exaggerating the metallic voice and rapping out questions with such grim precision that the contrast between the bot's meticulousness and Summers's fidgeting, hesitations, and backtrackings undermined his credibility. Julio had initially disliked Summers, but now he began to feel sorry for the man. He flipped down the headset's side flaps, and the lobby disappeared.

"Mr. Summers," intoned the prosecutor, "you claim that the Gen-K 3000 is capable of making decisions based on the data spectrum it amasses about its clients, yet you also propose that the client's desires fuel the generative component of the kitchen."

"Yes."

"Isn't that a contradiction?"

The defense bot raised its green hand. "Objection! Counsel has asked this question already! Innumerable times!"

"Overruled," said the judge.

Summers was sweating, and his once well-pressed suit hung limp. He mopped his brow and then crushed the handkerchief in his fist.

"No, it's not—I mean, I don't see it as—no, we." He took a deep breath. "*We* at Gen-K Corp don't think that's a contradiction. The Gen-K bonds with its owners, and that partnership grows more integrated—more complex—over time. The Gen-K takes the initiative, based on client data, and then performs whatever operation best suits that person's needs. But there's also client input, yes."

"In what form?"

"Like I said, through the voice commands, but also through the sum total of the biometrics." He smiled through gritted teeth. "The Gen-K knows you better than you know yourself."

"Well, sir, if that slogan is true, then wouldn't the Gen-K know if a woman *wanted* to kill her husband? Would it *act* on that input, even if she didn't give a specific voice command?"

Summers blanched.

"Answer the question," ordered the judge.

"Theoretically, yes," he stammered, "but practically, no—the Gen-K always acts in the best interests of its clients."

The prosecution bot swiveled its head. "But how would you define 'best interests'? What if Mrs. Ellis decided that her 'best interest' was to be free of her husband?"

Summers twisted his handkerchief and looked pleadingly at the jurycam. "But the Gen-K wouldn't kill a client! It's programmed to obey the law! So, even if a client wanted to commit murder, the Gen-K wouldn't comply. Plus, being dead wouldn't be in the best interest of Mr. Ellis, you know?"

The prosecution bot strolled away from the witness and stood caddy corner from Mrs. Ellis, who stared into space. "But Mr. Summers, what does a Gen-K do if the 'best interests' of its two most frequent users clash? How does it choose whose 'best interest' to serve?"

Summers shrugged. "I think that's a question for the techs, sir."

"But what is *your* opinion—based on knowledge of your company's product?"

Summers sunk his neck into his shoulders and wrinkled his nose, as if swallowing vinegar. "The Gen-K would give priority to the person it works with most often."

"No further questions, your honor," said the prosecutor.

Julio paused the vidstream and stretched. Remembering Iris, he inclined his body in her direction—but she was gone. He was so attentive to the trial that he hadn't noticed her departure. He scooted over to Iris's former spot and nestled into the warm groove in the cushions left by her torso. Her scent lingered.

The old woman lifted her headset and shot him a nasty glance. Annoyed at her fussiness, Julio kicked off his shoes and extended his legs onto the middle cushion, so that his feet were within an inch of the purse barrier. The old woman snorted, snatched up her purse, and left in a huff.

Closing his eyes, Julio massaged his temples and returned his thoughts to the trial. He was beginning to feel annoyed at both attorneys. The prosecution's witnesses had convinced him that Mrs. Ellis was guilty, but then Summers's testimony raised doubts in his mind. Now, after the prosecutor's cross-examination, he doubted those doubts and wondered if the defense bot could turn the case around again. He switched on the vidstream.

The defense bot approached the witness stand for the redirect examination. Summers leaned back, smoothed his lapels, and resumed his grin, clearly relieved to be rid of the prosecutor.

The green bot approached the stand. "Mr. Summers, you have testified that the Gen-K accumulates data on a client and then acts on that client's behalf."

"Yes, sir. I mean, ma'am."

"Let's remind the jury: would the Gen-K have known that George Ellis had pancreatic cancer?"

"Of course."

"Because of the biometrics."

"Yes. It probably would have known about the cancer even before Mr. Ellis did—that is, depending on when he visited his doctor for a check-up."

"Would the Gen-K have notified Mr. Ellis of his condition?"

"No—that's not its function. Our sister corporation, Gen-M, makes diagnostic machines for home use. The Gen-K 3000 is designed to make people happy—to create meals that please."

"So the Gen-K would prescribe healthy foods, if it determined that a person was sick?"

Summers sniffed in annoyance. "The Gen-K *always* serves healthy food—or else favorably modifies food that may be unhealthy."

The defense bot faced the jurycam. "Would the Gen-K have

known if Mr. Ellis were depressed as a result of receiving a cancer diagnosis?"

"The Gen-K's affect recognition technology is extremely accurate, so I would have to say that yes, it would know if a person was depressed, but, unlike a human being, it wouldn't speculate about the cause."

"If the depressed person had any thoughts of doing away with himself, would the Gen-K know that, too?"

Summers began to pick at a hangnail. Before he could answer, the prosecution bot sprang up. "Objection: speculation."

"Overruled," replied the judge.

"The Gen-K specializes in modeling desire, based on its readings of biometrics and affect," Summers continued. "So, yes, it would probably be able to gauge even, ah, unpleasant desires." He perked up. "But the Gen-K would respond by offering mood-enhancing food selections—like fish, almonds, chocolate, certain kinds of squash."

"But, for the record, the Gen-K would know not only if a client were depressed, but that he desired to die: not from his disease, but in a way that was relatively quick and painless."

Summers hesitated. The courtroom was silent, except for the faint hum of the jurycam. He gave the handkerchief a yank. "Yes."

Julio's doubts about the case—and about the effectiveness of the Vacation Jury system—intensified as the trial dragged on through the second week. Although the skies cleared and he could sit by the pool again, he paced the grounds and hotel corridors like a caged jaguar. With each round of the premises, he noticed ceiling cracks, walls discolored by sepia stains, and mold blooms overlaying the mosaicked lobby tiles.

Eventually, he knew the hotel so well that he could wander almost anywhere with his headset on, except for the exclusive penthouse floor, available only to jurors willing to pay for the upgrade to the basic resort package subsidized by the court. As he prowled the hallways and public areas, he began to see afterimages of the courtroom superimposed on the scene even when he wasn't wearing the equipment: green bots extemporizing in the palm fronds, and ranks of identical purple jurors, their yellow chest numerals golden in the sun, lounging in the Adirondack chairs by the pool—all to the tune of a slack stringed luau guitar.

Alert for Iris, he studied the other jurors and became expert at gauging how long they were prisoners in paradise. Jury groups just off the plane were ecstatic. Jurors who stayed beyond a week grew restless, and those whose trials stretched into three weeks or a month ceased to care about their appearances and haunted the lobby, cafeteria, and pool in pajamas or with lank, unwashed hair. Only Iris continued to look fresh to his eyes. But, as the second week lengthened into a third and then a fourth week, he saw her less often, despite his incessant pacing.

After his disastrous attempt to signal his room number to Iris with the cocktail coaster, she curtailed her evening beach walks, and he only caught occasional and unexpected glimpses of her crossing the lobby or sunning herself on the opposite side of the pool, her deck chair turned to face away from his room. Julio was certain that the guards must have warned her, as they had warned him, about the three strike rule and threatened her with expulsion. Nevertheless, every night at sunset he would stand bare-chested on the balcony, with stubborn hopes that she would appear. As the days lapsed into weeks, he began to think of his vigils not only as a protest to the guards—whom he knew would be watching him on their surveillance cameras—but as a memorial to the fun he and Iris had had together in trying to beat the system.

Her failure to show up for her evening walks convinced him that she must have found him attractive and that those walks during the first week signaled the intensity of her interest. So perhaps she might, still, take the initiative and visit his room some night. After all, she had seen the number on the coaster. If she were clever enough to outfox the guards, she might show up for a tryst—especially if she were only under penalty of a first strike, or maybe none at all if the guards had focused their spite on him for making advances toward her. Night after night, as he lay in bed, he listened for her knock on his door. After imagining the delights of what followed he would add other scenarios: he and Iris sneaking off together to go salsa dancing in Acapulco (Toni hated dancing); he and Iris deliberating together on the jury and sharing exactly the same perspective on the trial; he and Iris reuniting post-trial in Chicago, where, liberated at last from the silence of sequestration, they would bond over their love of 20th century screwball comedies and engage in snappy dialogue worthy of Gable and Lombard.

His fantasies of how he and Iris would subtly communicate during the deliberation phase varied as the trial unfolded. He tried to follow the testimony, but it seemed increasingly disjointed. The vidstream was heavily edited, and he assumed that the lawyers were wrangling over procedure, since the testimony consisted of so many jump cuts. The defense introduced a parade of witnesses, all technical experts on the generative kitchen, each with a different interpretation of the logs recorded on the night of George Ellis's death. The maintenance tech who serviced the Ellis's kitchen scrutinized the couple's user imprints in the Gen-K's memory. Security experts opined that the system could have been hacked to cause Mr. Ellis's death. After reviewing the kitchen's update logs, a programmer suggested that, because the Ellis kitchen was the International Model, it linked its legal databases to those in Europe, where euthanasia was legal. The last technical expert, a designer of the kitchen's neural net, revealed that the 3000's ability to model desire was a commercial application of newly declassified Department of Defense technology—a fact which the defense bot stretched to imply that the Gen-K 3000 was a killing machine because it was built on military software calibrated to turn a soldier's thoughts of exterminating an enemy into deadly drone fire.

The prosecutor's cross-examinations were protracted, with endless nitpicking over technical specs that went way over Julio's head. But the blue bot always came back to the same question: Did the kitchen have agency? Didn't it need input from its owner to act? The defense bot, on the other hand, always proposed the opposite: Mr. Ellis's death was the fault of the kitchen, and, by implication, the Gen-K Corporation, not Mrs. Ellis.

Trying to understand the testimony, Julio sat at the desk in his room every night after his balcony vigils and obsessively reviewed the vidtranscripts, clicking on his highlighter to bookmark the evidence he found most significant. He suspected that there would be a civil suit brought against Gen-K, and that the legal wrangling that made the vidstream so disjunctive had to do with what evidence about the kitchen was relevant to the Ellis trial. But, after weeks of listening to data about emergent behaviors in complex adaptive systems, he felt that the trial had lost its human element.

Julio's interest in the testimony improved at the end of the fourth week, when the defense summoned its last witness, George Ellis's personal physician, to the stand. Julio had heard that doctors who served the wealthy spent as much time visiting body sculptors as their clients did, and Dr. Leah Rittenhouse proved it. Toned and athletic, she radiated health. In a sober contralto, she reviewed the details of Mr. Ellis's physical and psychiatric history, confirming the diagnosis of pancreatic cancer and detailing her high-tech efforts to combat it through nano-guided radiation, chemo-insulin cocktails, gene resplicing, and tumor inhibiting angiogenesis. Julio was amazed that such resources were available to Mr. Ellis—not only on office visits, but at all. Julio had known several people at work who were unlucky enough to get cancer, but the insurance company provided by Allied Packaging always attributed the cancer to the victim's unhealthy lifestyle choices—especially the stress of working such long hours—and denied treatment.

"Dr. Rittenhouse," asked the green bot, "when did you inform Mr. Ellis that he had run out of options for a cure?"

"On what turned out to be his final appointment," she said, "the morning of September ninth, 2060, I informed the patient that his disease was terminal."

"And how did Mr. Ellis react?"

"As you can see from the diagnostics, his affect had wavered throughout the treatment year, and—"

"He was depressed?"

"Yes. Since being diagnosed in August 2059."

"Had you prescribed anything for the depression?"

"No. He told me that he didn't want to pay for anti-depressants when he had a remedy at home."

"And what remedy was that?"

"A generative kitchen. He trusted it to provide mood food."

"Did you agree with his plan?"

"Seratonin saturated meals, boosted by a generative kitchen, can be just as effective as anti-depressants."

"Did he have any other responses after his initial diagnosis?"

"He retired from his job. He also began patronizing a body sculpting studio."

"Did he tell you his reasons for these decisions?"

"Of course. I'm his affect manager, as well as his personal physician." She gave the bot an icy stare. "Major life changes are common after people learn they have a terminal illness. And sculpting is also not unusual: the patient gains confidence by changing aspects of his body—his external appearance—that he can control."

"Did he tell his wife about his diagnosis?"

"Not to my knowledge."

"Why not? Isn't it peculiar not to confide in one's spouse about major illness?"

"Not necessarily. Some people, especially men, see illness as a weakness, and choose to hide their condition. Since ninety percent of cancers are as curable as the common cold, many patients keep their status confidential."

"Did you advise Mr. Ellis to tell his wife?"

"Yes, but he rebuffed my suggestion."

"Did you discuss his options with him?"

"Yes. I gave him income-appropriate brochures for end-of-life services: luxury hospice suites or home specialists skilled in palliative care."

"So that he would experience little or no pain?"

"Yes."

"Did you discuss any other options with Mr. Ellis?"

The doctor glanced sideways toward the jurycam and raised her chin. "I broached only *legal* options."

"Did *Mr. Ellis* propose any other options?"

"Objection, your honor," interjected the prosecution bot. "Leading the witness."

"Overruled," said the judge bot. "Answer the question, doctor."

Dr. Rittenhouse squared her shoulders. "*Mr. Ellis* asked me if I could recommend any of the terminal tours of Europe."

"And did you?"

Her eyes flicked toward the jurycam again, then returned to the defense bot. "No, of course not. Advising a patient of that option is illegal."

"So you refused to discuss euthanasia with Mr. Ellis, as it is currently practiced, legally, in Europe?"

"Yes. I informed him of his *legal* options in *this* country: hospice and in-home end-of-life care."

"In your opinion, from what you know of Mr. Ellis's psychiatric profile, would he be the type of person to select that option— euthanasia in a luxury setting—if he could?"

The blue bot sprang up again. "Objection: speculation."

"Sustained," said the judge.

"The patients in your practice," said the defense bot, "all of them are financially well-off, correct?"

"I would say that most of them are in the top-five-percent income bracket, yes."

"Of your patients whose condition you deemed 'terminal,' how many left the country to, ah, voluntarily expire in Europe?"

Dr. Rittenhouse stiffened. "I keep no such statistics. I specialize in extending life. Few of my patients become 'terminal.'"

The defense bot nodded apologetically. "Of course, I understand. Nevertheless, despite advances in medical technology, all of us have to die eventually?"

"Yes," the doctor admitted.

"And it's also true that terminal patients of Mr. Ellis's considerable financial means often leave the country to take advantage of the legal option of euthanasia in the spas of Europe, particularly Switzerland?"

"As I said, I do not keep such statistics on my clients, but, yes, every year a significant percentage of terminal patients in Mr. Ellis's income bracket travel to the European spas."

"And Mr. Ellis repeatedly asked you about that option on September ninth, 2060?"

"Yes. But I would not advise him, due to the illegality of that option in this country. No, I would not."

"I understand. Thank you, Dr. Rittenhouse."

Julio loosened the straps on his headset and propped himself up in bed. He had camped in his room all day and ordered meals through room service. The prosecution bot had spent seven hours trying to undermine Doctor Rittenhouse, but she was a formidable opponent. After a brief redirect, the defense bot rested its case, and the judge bot announced that closing statements would be given the next day. The judge stressed that the jurors would have to check out of their rooms by 10:00 a.m. and watch the trial proceedings on a strict schedule, from 10:30 until 5:00, to be ready for the evening flight back to Chicago.

Flipping on the lights, Julio surveyed the piles of dirty t-shirts and underwear scattered across the floor. He hated the idea of returning home with a suitcase full of smelly clothes, but there was no time left for laundry. It was almost midnight, and he wanted to stroll on the beach once more before leaving.

He dragged himself from bed and slid open the balcony door. Heavy clouds blotted out the moon and stars and reflected back the city's lights in a dull glow. He hunched over the railing, massaging a crick in his back. A soft splash drew his attention to the pool. His eyes were still adjusting to seeing the world without the mediation of the vidscreen. He narrowed his gaze, trying to ignore the bot-colored flashes that interfered with the scene below. The lights on the pool patio were dim, but the water glimmered invitingly.

On the far side, drawing herself out with the help of the wide gutter, was Iris, naked. At least, he thought she was naked. He squinted and saw the faint outline of a thong against her hips as she leaned across a deck chair to grab a towel. He straightened, smoothing his hair back, and she turned to face him, giving him just a glimpse of her breasts, the nipples erect in the cool air, before she wrapped the towel around her torso. Squeezing the water from her braid, she met his gaze.

Julio tightened his hands around the railing. Iris paused and, still holding his gaze, opened the towel between her outstretched hands to dry her back. Although she had oriented herself so that the towel cast her body in shadow, Julio could still admire its ample curves, and how her hips swayed as she inched the towel down into the small of her back.

He tore his eyes away and glanced at the surveillance cameras above the tiki bar and lobby doors. Where were the guards? Had they made the same threats to her as they did to him? When he looked back at Iris, she had covered herself with the towel again. Making no pretense of avoiding detection, she flashed him a broad smile, tucked the top edge of the towel between her breasts, and strolled barefoot

43

towards the lobby.

Damn the surveillance cameras. If Iris was willing to break the rules, then he would too. He put his hand on the balcony door, calculating how much time it would take for him to run down to the pool area—or could he risk a swashbuckler move, like vaulting over the railing onto the concrete below? He hesitated, peering through the acrylic floor of the balcony to gauge the distance. When he raised his head, Iris was gone.

Julio hardly slept that night. He had dashed to the lobby to head off Iris and found no one there except for a dozing receptionist. He spent the rest of the night tossing and turning in bed, alternating between fantasies of caressing iridescent brown skin and fears of guards banging down his door.

When he woke, it was 9:30 a.m. Gusts of rain beat against the balcony door. He took a speed shower and crammed his suitcase full. By the time he got down to the lobby, all of the couches and chairs were taken, so he sat on his suitcase, back to the wall, to watch the closing statements.

There was no sign of Iris. Julio adjusted the headset's backscreen so that he could scan the lobby, and he grew increasingly worried as the hours passed and she failed to appear. Had the guards apprehended her because of her skinny dip?

At 2:00, the prosecution bot concluded its argument, a relentless portrayal of Mrs. Ellis as a cold-blooded, calculating murderer. His stomach growling, Julio stood and began to pace, aiming his headset toward the elevators in case Iris should emerge.

As he listened to the defense bot go into excruciating detail about every possibility for reasonable doubt, Julio increased the range of his pacing, drawing closer to the elevators at every turn. The Ellis jury was mandated to check out of their rooms and spend the day watching the closing statements in real time.

Iris must have been arrested and thrown off the jury.

He paused and sat down again on his suitcase. If Iris was guilty of violating the sequestration rules, then why had the guards spared him? Her behavior was much more brazen than his last night, but wasn't he complicit, even partially responsible? Should he take a similar risk for her?

He closed his eyes and tried to concentrate on the vidstream. The defense bot was arguing that in response to new technologies society should evolve new legal precedents: the jury needed to understand the ethical complexity of the Ellis case and not reduce it to the simplistic "black and white" terms that the prosecution proposed. As he listened, Julio envisioned Iris as a victim of affect recognition technology. The terms were straightforward enough. Iris had risked so much for him and taken the fall. But he was guilty, too.

He clenched his fists and stood up. His temples pounded, and he felt strung-out from lack of food and sleep. What was the ethical choice? He steadied himself against the wall and imagined sitting beside Iris on the plane to Chicago, both of them expelled from the jury and able to talk, at last.

As the defense bot swung into a final plea for finding Mrs. Ellis not guilty, the jurycam focused on her for an extended close-up. The composure she had maintained throughout the trial dissolved when the bot insisted that she should be spared the death penalty. Tears coursed down her cheeks and dripped onto her cardigan, but she kept her hands firmly clenched on the table. The jurycam tightened its focus on her, and she buried her head in her hands. The close-up faded, and an instruction list appeared on the screen. In a somber voice-over, the judge began to explain the deliberation protocols.

Julio switched off the headset. He surveyed the lobby and noticed a pair of female guards beside the reception desk, the only other people standing in a sea of jurors sprawled on the couches. The perfect stage for him to shout in protest and break the sequestration oath. It was his ethical duty to share the blame with Iris.

But before he could speak, the guards lunged for him. A few jurors took off their headsets and squinted as the guards guided him onto a bench near the elevator vestibule.

"Take it easy, Mr. González," said the first guard. "There's no reason to break the oath now. Trial's over. Deliberation will start soon after you return to Chicago."

Julio loosened his headset and wiped the sweat from his brow. "But it's not fair. Why arrest her and not me?"

The guards exchanged glances.

"No one from your jury has been arrested, Mr. González," the second guard said. "But you came close a few minutes ago. Our affect recognition technology prevented you from committing your third strike."

"If no one's been arrested, then where is she?" Julio stripped off the headset and flung it on the floor.

A bell pinged and the gilded doors to the penthouse elevator rolled open. Iris emerged, clad in a leopard print dress and stiletto heels. A porter followed, pushing a cart laden with designer suitcases. Giving no sign of recognition, she breezed by Julio and the guards.

Julio lifted a hand to signal to her, and the second guard gently guided it back to his lap.

"Do you need a new incentive to maintain the sequestration rules?" said the first guard, handing him a bill. "Here's the total for your Vacation Resort stay, including room and board, airfare, and amenity fees."

Julio scrutinized the bill. "But this adds up to twice my yearly wages! The bill you showed me three weeks ago was far less—"

"Perhaps the night shift failed to explain. The fee rate quadruples with each strike."

"Punitive resort charges?"

"That's right."

Julio felt dizzy. "Did she face punitive charges?" He pointed at Iris, who stood several yards apart from the jurors queuing for the airport shuttle.

"Of course," said the guard, "but she didn't come as close as you just did to breaking the rules." She winked. "We're required to give a bit more leeway to our penthouse customers."

The hours between the trip to the airport and take-off blurred in Julio's mind. The guards had given him an energy bar, which settled his stomach but must have contained a mild sedative. He felt disengaged from the scene around him as they hustled him onto the shuttle. The rain had stopped, but the van's windows were fogged. He rubbed a clear space on the pane and caught a glimpse of Iris stepping into a limousine.

On the plane, she disappeared into the first class cabin. For Julio and the other coach passengers, boarding was excruciating. Accommodating many juries, the flight was full, and the attendants had drawn up a complicated seating chart that situated jurors from the same trial several rows apart from one another. Squeezed into his window seat beside an enormous woman, Julio watched the jurors shuffle through the plane's narrow aisle. He tried to count the people he recognized, to see how many he could identify who were likely his jury mates, but stopped when the old woman, clutching her bulging straw purse, paused to look daggers at him before she settled into an aisle seat two rows ahead of him. Although he itched to begin discussing the trial, he did not relish the prospect of dealing with her.

After the plane reached cruising altitude, Julio fidgeted and guessed that the sedative must have worn off. His stomach lurched every time the plane changed altitude. But his fear of flying was nothing compared to the anxiety he began to feel about closing his eyes, for whenever he tried to sleep, he saw not the afterimages of bots that had haunted him in the hotel, but Mrs. Ellis.

Relaxing his grip on the armrests, Julio unwedged his body from the cramped seat, turned toward the window, and froze when he saw the apparition of Mrs. Ellis reflected there, her wispy gray hair framing her forehead like a halo. She returned his stare, tears rimming her eyes, and he felt embarrassed, as if he had invaded her privacy. His face flushed, and he looked away, unsure of whether he was asleep or hallucinating. He flicked his eyes open to find a flight attendant leaning toward him, her face spring green in the cabin's half light. She asked whether he wanted coffee or tea.

"Not guilty," he murmured, and felt certain for the first time in weeks. All the doubts he had harbored during the second half of the trial converged to convince him that Mrs. Ellis had not murdered her husband.

"Did you say 'tea,' sir?" asked the flight attendant.

"Ah—sure. Yes, fine." He set the warm plastic cup on his tray table and fell into a dreamless sleep.

The court granted them a day to get resettled in Chicago. Too exhausted to complain to any of the officials who herded them off the plane, escorted them to the baggage carousels, and shunted them into Vacation Jury Courtesy Vans, Julio thought that the court's definition of "day" was questionable, given that the flight was a red-eye. They arrived at 9:00 a.m. and had to appear at the Deliberation Center twenty-four hours later.

But Julio did not arrive back at his micro-apt until that afternoon. Despite its welcoming logo—"Court E-Z" in pink letters arcing over justice scales plumped on a pillow—the van was designed to squeeze in sixteen jurors and their luggage, far too many to make the ride comfortable for anyone but the driver in his ergonomic seat. The van left just at the end of morning rush hour and just at the start of a blizzard. Navigating the slippery streets, the driver went at a pace that Julio would have described as tropical if they were back in Acapulco. Conveying jurors to different locations all over the city, he took no short cuts, but inched the unwieldy van along designated snow routes, where the traffic was alternately blocked by enormous plows and by tow trucks dragging away stalled cars. As the next-to-last juror to be dropped off, Julio was grateful to have the option to decline a courtesy ride to the South Side Deliberation Center for the next morning.

He dragged his suitcase up three flights of stairs and staggered into his drafty micro apartment, now more frigid than usual because the driver had only just given him the code that would, with court-mandated restrictions, revive his phone. Kicking the suitcase into a corner, he switched on the phone and initiated the control to raise his unit's thermostat and flush-and-fill the nutrient paste dispenser in the food printer.

Then, he checked his messages. Twelve thousand? All but one marked "URGENT"? In keeping with his juror service contract, he had given the court permission to cut off all his media streams until the trial's conclusion and to limit his contacts to three "essential," court-approved people: his mom, Toni, and Shea, his boss. He had balked at the idea of listing Shea, but she had insisted he check in with her after he returned to Chicago and then keep her posted about when he expected to be back on the job.

Scrolling through the messages, he cursed. All of the "URGENT" ones were work orders: delinquent packaging insurance claims auto-forwarded, for his "immediate attention," by Shea. He tried to sort through the messages to determine how many were original, and how many were Allied Packaging Insurance Company "URGENT REMINDER" notices generated by the system computer when an employee took too much time dealing with a work order, but he soon gave up. Evil bitch. Knowing Shea expected at least a vidconference, he drafted a simple text: "Had gr8 time in Acapulk! Xpect delib 2 take weeks!" He signed the text with a smiley face wearing sunglasses, pressed "send" with his middle finger, and grinned.

He yawned, pulled up the phone's menu app for the food printer, and punched in a request for a stack of maple-flavored nutrient paste pancakes. His stomach rumbling at the smell of frying batter, he unfolded the built-in table from the wall, drew the comfier of his two chairs beside it, and sat down to search the inbox for the one message not marked "urgent."

The subject line read: "Marathon Girl Misses U." A vidmessage from Toni. The still photo she chose as a teaser showed her smiling, sleek and sweaty in her running togs. She must have trained hard in his absence, her usual way of working through anger, although she usually hated winter training. His thumb hovered over the initiate button. He was curious about what she would say, but did not want to be drawn into any emotional b.s. right now. He was too tired to want to deal with finalizing the break-up with Toni. They had been dating long enough that he did not want to just text her goodbye. He would need to tell her face-to-face—he owed her that much—which would mean he ought to make a date to meet with her, which would be tantamount to scheduling another tedious argument. Even a vidcall would be a chore. No, he would wait until the trial was done to get in touch with Toni.

But he did need to call his mom. Behind him, the food printer pinged, and he twisted in his chair to plate a tall stack of pancakes and grab a beer from the micro-fridge's beverage port. He plopped the meal on the table, tucked the phone into the slot on the opposite wall so that he could eat and talk, said "call mom," and began tearing the top pancake into bite-sized pieces.

"Julio!" She beamed at him from the screen.

Her salt-and-pepper hair and gentle laugh lines startled him for a moment. Had she aged since they last talked? Or had his view of women in their fifties been skewed by watching hours of testimony from Mrs. Ellis's ultra-sculpted friends?

"Hey, Mom." He smiled back, hoping he looked happy and relaxed.

"When did you get back?"

"The trip was great. Gorgeous resort. You would have loved it. The sunsets especially."

Her smile turned rueful. "I'm sure it's just as beautiful as Havana. What's left of it, anyway."

Julio thought of consoling her by saying the dike that saved Acapulco had obliterated the beach view of the ocean horizon, but decided to avoid evoking further memories of the Cuban coastline being washed away. "Have you heard from the cousins there recently?"

"We haven't spoken in years—my Spanish is rusty—but I'd make the trip if I could. Family is family." She paused for a sip of tea. "So. Tell me about the trial."

"I can't. The court won't allow it."

"How would they know?"

"Trust me, they would." Julio was itching to tell her everything, but he assumed the court officials had installed a call surveillance program on his phone.

"Can't you at least tell me the charges? Was it murder?"

Time for a diversion. He took a swig of beer, dipped his head so it was just out of range of the phonecam, tucked a piece of pancake into his mouth, and began chewing.

"Julio! Are you eating with your fingers again?"

He brought his head up level with the phonecam. "C'mon Mom. Nobody's here to be insulted."

"Toni's not with you?"

"I'm still sequestered."

"But they let married people see each other—"

"We're not married, Mom."

"Well, you've been dating long enough."

Score one for Mom. Was she criticizing the courts or insinuating that he and Toni should get married? He decided not to ask. He took another swallow of beer and waited.

"Does your sequestration mean you won't be able to come for Sunday dinner?" his mom continued. "Everyone will be there. You don't spend enough time with your nephews."

Julio closed his eyes and massaged his temples. He had no idea what day of the week it was. He opened his eyes and considered touching the screen to check the calendar, but felt too exhausted to move. "Mom. I have to debilitate—no, deliberate. Trial's not over until we reach a verdict."

"You deliberate on Sundays?!"

"Maybe. We had to stream the trial on weekends."

"What kind of vacation is that? I thought you said you had a wonderful time?"

"I did."

"You must be starved for a real Chicago pizza. Do you want me to order sausage or pepperoni this Sunday?"

"That sounds great, Mom. But really, I won't be able to come until the trial is over. And I need to sleep now."

"Be good to yourself, Julio. Don't take everything so seriously. Be sure to go out for a walk once the sidewalks get cleared. That apartment is too small for you."

"Love you, Mom. I'll call again soon."

He waved, signed off before she could say anything more, and rested his head in his arms on the table.

The sound of a snowplow outside jolted him awake. The apartment was dark. He touched his phone to check the time: 6:00 p.m. Steadying himself as he stood, he considered grabbing a chair cushion for his head and stretching out on the floor for the night. But sleeping slumped on the table had given him a backache, so he knew he had to prep the bed. He took a last swallow of beer, stuffed the plate of pancakes into the mini-fridge, and flipped the table upside down to bed mode. Already nostalgic for the ease of hotel living, he unpacked sheets, pillows, and his microfiber quilt from their wall cubbies, made the bed, stripped off his clothes, and crawled in.

Huddled beneath the quilt, Julio listened to the plow blundering along the street and wondered whether the blizzard would smother the city enough that deliberation would be postponed. As he sunk into sleep, the snowflakes fell so fast that they buried the plow entirely, flowed up his building's stairs, and turned into twelve thousand work orders—the paper kind, like in the movies. In a white whirl they multiplied and surged around his bed. He heard a runner, steps pounding along the sidewalks—had they been cleared already?—but the drifts crested and he threw off the quilt and stood on the lurching bed to signal for help. He shielded his eyes against the glare, searching the horizon.

Hearing a splash, he turned and beheld Iris, naked except for a lei of gardenias and dried chile peppers, rising just off the port side of his bed. Her rainbow colors shone in sharp definition, a beacon against the monotony of white. Smiling, she took his hand and guided him into her shell-shaped boat. He tore off the lei, the chiles searing his fingertips, drew her down on the blossom strewn deck, kissed her gratefully, and ran his hands along her torso. As he pressed his body against hers, warm color suffused his skin, separating into rainbow bands that shimmered in tune with hers: the reds pepper-hot, the greens cool as absinthe on ice. The sea swelled, lifting their boat to the top of the Acapulco Dike, then over and down into the violent turquoise bay.

A strange ringtone jolted him awake. The apartment was pitch black, lit only by the phone blinking in its slot. Julio reached up, groped along the wall above his head, and tapped the phone to silence it. He rolled over and sunk back to sleep.

The phone chimed again, at increased volume. Julio sat, tore it off the wall, and checked the time. 6:05 a.m. Had he set an alarm last night? He silenced the phone and sat listening, hearing nothing outside except for a lone car moving down the street, its progress muffled by snow. He lay down, shoved the phone under his extra pillow, and slept.

The phone went off a third time, the cloying Big Ben tune now followed by a cheerful jingle: "RISE AND SHINE, DELIBERATION AT NINE!" He shook himself awake, pulled the phone from beneath the pillow, and checked the time. 6:30. He dragged himself into the bathroom, slid the phone under a stack of towels, and returned to bed, where he drifted in and out of sleep until weak slivers of sunlight flickered through the venetian blinds.

The building door slammed—a neighbor, leaving for work—and Julio forced himself out of bed. In the bathroom, he groped under the towels and withdrew the phone, now buzzing in a high pitched whine like an angry mosquito and blinking the time at a frantic pace: 7:45. He tapped the phone, then shook it, but could not turn off the damned alarm.

"Alright," he shouted, "I'm up, leave me alone!"

The phone went mute. He dropped it on the vanity and contemplated it warily. He had agreed to let the court limit and monitor his calls, but not the alarm program. What else could the phone sense? Was the court tracking him?

They must know he was running late. No time for a shower. But he would not face Iris across the deliberation table without, at least, a shave.

Cursing the unwieldiness of his high-tech twelve-bladed safety razor, Julio rushed the chore and cut his chin twice.

Increasingly anxious about seeing Iris, he splashed aftershave on his cheeks, pulled on tight-fitting slacks and a blue silk shirt, and shoved his feet into waterproof dress boots.

His thoughts veered between afterimages of his dream and sober recollections of Iris brushing him off two days ago in Acapulco. He felt chastened enough that he did not plan to approach her, but he hoped he looked decent enough. If she operated under a looser set of sequestration rules, then he would let *her* make the first move.

He studied his reflection in the mirror. If she was the type of girl to buck the system, then he had no doubt she would side with him and agree that Mrs. Ellis was a victim of technological circumstance. As deliberation proceeded, he would impress her with his command of the evidence.

Pressed for time, he wolfed down a cold pancake, skipped brewing coffee, and dashed outside. The snow had stopped, but the icy sidewalks were hard to navigate. On the express El downtown, he stood sweating in his winter coat, packed in a crowd of commuters, all of them peering at their phones. Julio wondered how the Bulls had done in his absence and was tempted to ask the man wedged beside him, but held back. He had no idea whether his phone, tucked in his shirt pocket, was now sensitive enough to record even an innocuous sports conversation and forward it to the courts, but he did not want to risk being thrown off the trial now, when he was so close to engaging with Iris face-to-face.

Or risk having his wages garnished, he thought as the train accelerated up the steep ramp to the precipitous third level tracks, built to accommodate the latest generation of tornado-proof skyscrapers, and approached the Wells Street stop, where he usually got off for work. He mentally gave the finger to Shea and glanced at the ads flashing on the vidscreens overhead: teaser rates for the holoslot salons at the Federal casinos; a new generation of food printers capable of synthesizing vegetable proteins; and an invitation, promising prizes galore, for people to enter the Mile High Marathon—a race up and down the stairways of the DelivRite Drone Building on Wacker Drive.

The marathon ad showed the blocky outline of the old, 20th century tower, once the tallest building in the world, now festooned with drone ports. Julio began speculating about how many of his outstanding claims he could source to that building alone. DelivRite claims were the worst. The corporation had the monopoly on drone deliveries throughout the city and always cut corners on packaging. Its tracking system was so byzantine that Julio and his co-workers often joked that the drones must be programmed to fly loose in the enormous tower before setting skyward on their delivery runs.

Hustling to exit at the Jackson street platform, Julio cursed the ad for making him think about work—and Toni. He had no doubts that she would have ponied up to enter the Mile High Marathon, no matter the cost. She would be overjoyed to have a winter training goal—especially one he would find annoying. He always griped as she approached marathon deadlines, because she focused more on the race than on him. Slouching on the escalator to street level, he imagined her dodging escaped drones as she toiled up building's endless staircases.

He transferred to a plodding South Side bound bus and distracted himself with fantasies of ditching his micro apartment and moving in with Iris. If she were wealthy enough to afford the penthouse upgrade at the resort, then surely she would have a swank condo, maybe in one of the towers on Lake Shore Drive. Gazing out the window towards the lake, he tried to be realistic. Would Iris think he was a drone because he spent his working hours trying to wrest settlement claims from DelivRite?

Muffled by his coat, the mosquito whine sounded. He jerked to attention and saw that the bus was approaching the Deliberation Center stop. He fished out the phone and tapped the screen furiously. People stared. At the stop, the alarm rose to an ear-splitting pitch and only ceased when he stepped onto the Deliberation Center's sidewalk.

After dodging snowplows in the plaza, he made his way through the security line and presented himself at the Room Assignment counter, which looked suspiciously like the hotel's checkout desk. A bored clerk gave him a room number, keypad code, and instruction pod. Julio made his way to the elevator and at the forty-second floor stepped out into an ill-lit corridor. The doors were spaced so closely that he wondered how the court could fit so many deliberation rooms on one floor. But when he stepped inside his assigned room, he understood: he faced a virtual reality console.

Flipping on the lights, he dialed into his instruction pod. A perky female voice informed him that, to promote fairness in deliberations, all jury activity was mandated to take place behind the guise of video sims styled as the bots used in the trial. Along with giving standardized instructions for operating the console, the voice informed him that keeping the jurors isolated in separate rooms prohibited "extracurricular discussion" of the case, and the computer-generated bots would prevent the jurors from judging one another on the basis of gender, race, age, or appearance.

"Justice is blind, and jurors should be, too!" said the voice. As if anticipating his impulse to flee, it cheerfully reminded Julio of the penalties associated with juror delinquency: fines totaling double the cost of the resort fees and imprisonment for non-payment.

Julio sighed and sat down at the console, placing the helmet over his head and his hands on the control wands, whose stickiness reminded him that he had neglected to buy a coffee at the kiosk downstairs. He activated the keypad on the dashboard, and, on the vidscreen, gazed through the eyes of his sim. Eleven purple bots sat around an oblong table, each with a yellow number on its chest. Their heads swiveled toward him.

"About time, Number Five," said bot Number One from the head of the table. "The court's tracking monitor said you were on the way, but you took so long we were just about to call in one of the alternates."

"Come on, cut him some slack," said Number Six. "Aren't all the Court-E-Z vans running late due to the snow? Mine was."

Julio stared at the VR dashboard, unsure of what to say.

"Maybe he needs time to figure out the VR system," said Number Three.

"Where's he been living for the past century, a hole in the ground?" said Number Two.

Julio tried to respond, but the controls were so primitive that there was a lag between his command and the sim's screen response. The best he could do was to make his bot's mouth hang open.

Bot Number Eleven leaned back in its chair and crossed its arms. "These VR consoles must be several decades old—maybe Five is too young to remember them. I, for one, wish that we had the chance to dress up our sims."

"Maybe the court should provide some training before throwing us into these cubicles," suggested Number Seven. "You know, 'Retro Sim 101'?"

"They just want to herd us in and out as fast as possible," said Number Nine. "They don't give a damn about our comfort, or about whether the jury system makes any sense."

"How can you say that after having spent five weeks in Acapulco at their expense?" said Seven.

Julio fiddled with the controls and realized that the volume was dampened on the vocalizer.

"Well, I vote for getting us in and out of here as fast as possible," said Number Eleven. "And this guy's slowing us down." It turned to Julio. "Or are you a girl?"

"Silence," said Number One. "We're not supposed to divulge that information. It's prejudicial."

"Do we really need to hear that warning again?" countered Eleven. "Maybe some so-called prejudicial information is relevant: I'm eighty-five and proud of it. With age comes wisdom—"

"And maybe there are jurors here older than you," said Number One, "but I trust that no one else will reveal their age. This isn't a competition."

Julio finally brought the voice function online. "I apologize for being late," he ventured, hating the way the vocalizer changed the rich timbre of his voice from baritone to monotone. "I thought we were going to meet one another face-to-face."

"The judge explained that after the closing statements," said Number Eleven. "Or were you floating somewhere on a tiki raft?"

Several of the bots snickered.

"He said he was sorry," said Seven. "Or she. So let's get on with it."

"Okay," said Number One. "Excuse me while I read the instructions here in my cubicle." The bot's body froze on the screen, while the voice continued. "We're supposed to start with an icebreaker."

"We've been sitting here for forty minutes," said Number Eleven. "The ice is broken already. In fact, there's a huge crevasse, and it's growing wider every second. Let's talk about the trial."

"No," insisted Number One. "I'm the Foreperson, and I'm supposed to see that we do everything by the book. We have to—we're being recorded."

Julio manipulated his bot's head to view the room and noticed cameras poised in every corner.

"Yeah, despite the court's efforts to economize, it's interesting to observe what they choose to simulate in this V- room," remarked Seven.

"Alright," said One, "we'll count the pleasantries we exchanged while waiting for Number Five as our icebreaker. The next step is to hold a preliminary vote."

"Fine," said Eleven, "That shouldn't take long. The woman is quite obviously guilty."

"The vote will be taken privately," continued One, "by pressing the 'yes' or 'no' button on your console. Red for 'yes,' green for 'no.'"

At the Foreperson's signal, they all voted. A huge scorescreen lit at the head of the room. Julio's heart sank when he saw the results: eleven for "Guilty," versus his solitary vote for "Not Guilty."

"So who's the holdout?" asked Six.

Julio froze at the controls, suddenly glad that he was anonymous.

Number Eleven broke the silence. "Well, whoever you are, if you're too chicken to stand up for your vote, then why not change it so we can get the hell out of here?"

"Yeah," said Ten, "Let's have a revote."

"Hang on," said Number One. "The rules say that if the vote is uneven, we have to deliberate."

"So who is it?" asked Six. "C'mon, speak up."

Julio raised his sim's hand, and all the others turned toward him.

Although their faces were featureless, he could have sworn that they looked at him accusingly.

"How can you possibly think she's innocent?" asked Two.

The other bots nodded.

"And how can you assume that she's guilty?" challenged Julio.

The bots all started talking at once, their monotone voices indistinguishable from one another, until Number One waved. "Calm down. Let's hear what Number Five has to say, and then we can offer our counterarguments."

"What's to argue?" said Eleven.

"We have to convince her to change her mind," said Seven. "The vote must be unanimous."

"Silence," said Number One. "Number Five, please explain your vote. Why do you think that McConnery Ellis is not guilty of murdering her husband?"

Julio flushed, feeling his face and fingers tingle as adrenalin surged through him. "Didn't any of you pay attention to the testimony? To the defense's closing arguments? Or to the judge's instructions that, because the death penalty is involved, we've got to be absolutely certain of our decision, 'beyond a reasonable doubt'?"

"I have no doubts," said Eleven.

"Nor do I," said Six.

The other bots nodded in agreement.

"Hey, if machines are self-aware enough to commit murder, then why aren't they sitting on this damned jury instead of us?" proposed Two, and the other bots laughed.

"It's not funny," said Julio. "Unlike Europe, we still have the death penalty. We can't just vote guilty and condemn Mrs. Ellis to be euthanized if there are so many other possible explanations for Mr. Ellis's death."

"She doesn't seem to take much interest in living if she's not willing to do any body sculpting," said Eleven.

"What does that have to do with whether or not she's guilty?" said

Julio.

"As I see it," ventured Seven, "the question is whether a machine, the kitchen, had enough agency to kill Mr. Ellis on its own, without any input from Mrs. Ellis. Frankly, I'm not convinced that it did. Therefore, I voted 'Guilty.'"

Julio turned his sim toward Seven, grateful that someone was willing to move the discussion in a rational direction. "Okay, but what about the defense's suggestion that the input was from *Mr. Ellis*? That the kitchen picked up on his desire to end his life in a Swiss spa?"

"And the machine kindly decided to spare him the expense?" cut in Number Six. "I think not."

"No, that's not the point," said Julio. "Don't you remember what Summers and the others said? The Gen-K took biometrics and affect readings of Mr. Ellis several times a day."

Number One stirred, as if waking from a doze. "If I may speak on behalf of my fellow jurors, no one doubts that Mr. Ellis was terminally ill. But we have no idea whether he had decided to, ah, terminate himself in Europe. The defense didn't offer any evidence that he'd made up his mind about end-of-life care."

"But don't you see," Julio countered, "if this is all a matter of interpretation, rather than a decision based on hard facts, then we should vote 'Not Guilty' and spare Mrs. Ellis."

"I think that most of us are basing our decisions on the facts," said Number Seven.

"So am I," said Julio. "Isn't it possible that the kitchen chose to euthanize Mr. Ellis because it was programmed to do what it determined was in the best interests of his health and well-being? Remember its mandate: 'the Gen-K knows you better than you know yourself'?"

"Are you really naïve enough to believe that marketing crap?" said Number Eleven.

"Didn't you pay attention to all of that testimony about the generative kitchen's capabilities?" said Julio.

"Sure, but I didn't believe it," said Eleven. "Like I said, it was all marketing hokum."

"Hokum?" asked Julio, unsure of what the word meant.

"Smoke and mirrors, kiddo," said Eleven.

"Number Eleven, please be civil," said Number One.

"Fine, but let's focus on the basic problem with our esteemed colleague Five's premise," responded Eleven. "If a kitchen wanted to kill someone, wouldn't it get violent? I mean, it doesn't face the death penalty like a human, so why would it be subtle enough to use cyanide laced almonds?"

"That's ridiculous," said Seven. "Why shouldn't we presume that, if it could kill, it would use the most ordinary means and do what it was designed to do—cook and bioengineer food?"

"But doesn't it do other things that are routinely dangerous?" said Eleven. "Let's see: it could mangle someone in the dish crusher."

"Burn someone with hot water, or with a gas flame," suggested Nine.

"Slice and dice with its knives," proposed Six.

"Asphyxiate Ellis with the oven gas," said Ten.

"Now hold on," said Seven. "We're getting away from the problem of whether the kitchen has agency."

"Not at all," said Eleven. "I think that all of this generative stuff is mere advertising, a set-up aimed to snooker the buyer. Like when I was a kid, I had one of those talking teddy bears that seemed to say the right thing at the right time, but when I got older I saw that I was only projecting onto it: convincing myself that its comments were relevant. I propose that the kitchen works just like that."

"You said you were eighty-five," Julio interjected. "So that was over seventy-five years ago. Don't you recognize that technology has changed since then? Aren't you the one being naïve?"

Eleven sat back in its chair and opened its hands expansively. "Smoke and mirrors, kiddo. Smoke and mirrors."

"I'm not ready to change my vote," said Seven. "But I don't like your logic, Eleven. If you think the Gen-K is a hoax, then how do you explain all the evidence we heard about it, including the testimony of witnesses like Mrs. Parker, who experienced its ability to make independent decisions?"

"Of course I know that technology has come a long way—I mean, look where we're sitting. But I also think the old marketing rules hold true: you've got to believe that you get what you pay for."

Julio wished the VR program would allow him to show the annoyance in his voice. "So how does that make Mrs. Ellis guilty of murder?"

"Well, why would she make such an illogical decision to get a kitchen in the first place, instead of choosing the body sculpting, like any rational woman would?"

"Because she liked to cook," said Seven. "That seemed clear from the testimony."

"But wouldn't we all agree that she could benefit from some serious bodywork?" said Eleven.

The bots all nodded.

"That's not the point," said Julio. "Come on, weren't you in the same courtroom as I was?"

"What courtroom?" said Six. "I was in a deckchair."

"I preferred the lobby couches," said Three.

"Me, too," said Twelve. "That hotel was cheap, but thank God they didn't skimp on the lobby air-conditioning."

"I sat on the balcony most of the time," admitted Nine. "My room faced seaside—the breeze was divine!"

"Come on, folks, let's get serious," said One, standing up again. "Number Five is asking—legitimately, I think—whether you all paid attention to your vidscreens while at the hotel."

"Thank you, Number One," said Julio.

"Now wait a minute," snapped Eleven. "I am serious. I'm not denying that Mrs. Ellis liked to cook. I'm just saying that by getting a generative kitchen, she could have had that and the bodywork, too: by murdering her husband."

"So you think her motive was bodywork?" asked Seven. "That's absurd."

"The motive, my dear, was money. Just like in the movies."

"Don't patronize me," said Seven. "And this is a real trial, with a real person's life at stake. Not a movie."

"Fine," said Eleven. "Then listen: here's my theory. She got the kitchen so that she could use it—including all of that b.s. about the generative stuff—to kill her husband and pretend the kitchen did it. Then she'd inherit the estate, have the bodywork done, and—voilÁ! Life begins at fifty—especially when a gal looks twenty-five! She could change her age, her shape, even her skin color as easily as changing her clothes. If only she had the money."

"But Mr. Ellis had terminal cancer," insisted Julio. "She would have inherited the estate anyway. So how could money have been her motive?"

"Yes," said Seven. "That was one point I found insightful in the defense's closing statement. Of course, it's still possible that the murder was a crime of passion. According to Mrs. Parker, the Ellises had a blow-up on the afternoon of his death."

"Hang on," said Eleven. "Remember that her friends and also the doctor all said that he hadn't told her yet about the cancer?"

"But can we be sure?" said Julio. "Maybe that came out in the argument."

"This is all speculation," said Six. "Why don't we get back to the basic question that those lawyer bots kept repeating. Was the kitchen capable of murder? Didn't it need some human input?"

Julio shouted into the vocalizer, but his voice came out as a monotone. "Yes—don't you see? The input came from the kitchen's readings of *Mr. Ellis!*" He shook the VR controls. "We're back to where we started!"

The Number One bot rose. "I propose that we take a break. If you look at the clock in the corner of your vidscreens, you'll see that it's way past lunchtime. Be back in one hour. Then we'll take another vote and see where we stand."

The screen dimmed. Still clutching the controls, Julio slumped over the console. He took off the helmet, grabbed his coat, and peered into the hall, expecting to see his fellow jurors emerge from their cubicles. But the corridor was empty, and so was the elevator. With sixty floors, the Deliberation Center likely housed thousands of VR cubicles, enough to keep jurors on the same trial far apart from one another.

In the crowded lobby, he stopped at one of the food kiosks for a sandwich and wolfed it down. Despite the cold, he needed to escape the building. When he got outside, he discovered that the sidewalks had been cleared of snow. Stuffing his hands into his pockets, he hunched against the wind and walked around the block, determined to work off his anger.

The cold air helped him think. How could he convince people who had already made up their minds? Who hadn't paid attention to the trial? And which one was Iris? Surely she, of all of the jurors, would be in sync with him. He wished that he had heard her speak at the resort, so that he could recognize something distinctive about her language amidst the bots' chatter. The only bot who took the time to reason out a decision was Number Seven. As he increased his speed along the sidewalk, Julio held the bot in his mind's eye and began to superimpose Iris's features over the generic purple head: the bronze braid, the sly smile, the eyes that spoke to him. Gaining new confidence with each step, he mentally pitched his argument to her. By the time he climbed the entryway's marble steps, he felt ready to begin again.

He arrived at the cubicle early, hoping to make small talk with Seven, but the screen remained dead until 2:30 p.m., the time that the Foreperson had designated for the jurors to reappear.

"Welcome back," said Number One, as the room rematerialized.

"My electronic roster informs me that everyone is present. Before we launch into discussion again, I'm calling for a second vote—"

"—to see if Five has come to its senses and changed its mind over lunch?" said Eleven.

"It's just a formality, Number Eleven," said One.

Julio voted and checked the scorescreen, hoping that his arguments that morning had influenced his peers. The vote remained locked at eleven to one.

He gripped the controls and tried to maneuver his bot into making an expansive gesture, but the bot just flapped its hands. "Why are you all so quick to condemn Mrs. Ellis?"

"The trial lasted over a month," said Six. "What's quick about that?"

"So you assumed she was guilty from the beginning?"

"Sure," said Six. "The prosecution's evidence was solid."

"I thought so too," said Julio, "until the defense offered so many valid reasons to believe the case wasn't open-and-shut."

"Valid reasons?" scoffed Eleven. "I would say the defense bot wasted my time, except that I was in Acapulco."

"That defense lawyer was all over the map," said Nine.

"Yeah," said Two. "The trial was just blather after the green bot took over."

"But what about all the questions the defense raised?" challenged Julio. "There's security—the kitchen could have been hacked. Or it could have fallen back into its basement DOD mode—the military software substrate, designed for killing. And the kitchen's affect recognition technology was state-of-the-art: it must have known if Mr. Ellis had decided in favor of a terminal tour."

"All of that 'expert' testimony was mumbo-jumbo," said Number Eight, and many of the bots nodded in agreement. "Having a human commit the crime makes more sense."

"Just because you think it makes more sense doesn't mean it happened that way!" said Julio, tweaking the volume control for emphasis.

"Isn't that what we're being asked to decide?" said Number Three.

"Yes, but we need to base our decision on reason—to weigh the evidence," said Julio.

"Are you accusing us of being stupid?" said Eleven. "I'm a rational person, which enables me to know that McConnery Ellis was highly *irrational* to choose a kitchen over bodywork, especially given her looks and age. So she must have had an ulterior motive for getting that kitchen."

"But that's just speculation," countered Julio.

"And it's not speculation to assume the kitchen magically murdered Mr. Ellis? What, you want us to think the kitchen felt sorry for him and decided to put him out of his misery? If you say that's rational, I say you're a fool!"

"Please be civil, Number Eleven," said Number One. "Being in a virtual environment doesn't give jurors the license to insult each other."

"Let me mediate," offered Number Seven. "Why don't we grant, for the sake of argument, that the kitchen was capable of intuiting Mr. Ellis's desires, and that Mr. Ellis accepted he was dying but wished to die quickly and painlessly."

"I'll grant you nothing. Mrs. Ellis is guilty. Period," said Number Eleven at high volume.

"Just listen, then. Let's agree—"

"But I don't agree."

"—*hypothetically*," insisted Seven, "that dying quickly and painlessly was in Mr. Ellis's best interests."

"I think the rest of us—except Eleven—can agree with you, hypothetically," said Number One. "What's your point, Seven?"

"Well, even if we accept all of those things," said Seven, "I don't believe that a major corporation like Gen-K would create a client-killing machine."

"So you believed Summers's hype?" asked Julio.

"Yes. The machine may have been programmed to act in its clients' best interests, but it's certainly not in the company's best interests to have a dead client. That's a contradiction that I can't get around."

"Yes," added Two, "that Summers guy kept saying over and over that the kitchen wasn't programmed to do anything illegal. And murder is illegal."

"Right," said Seven. "But so is euthanasia in this country. So even if we assume that the kitchen responded to Mr. Ellis's illness, and to his conscious or unconscious desires, and determined that a delicious, poisonous meal would be the best possible way to end his life, the programming couldn't have fulfilled that directive. According to the techs, the kitchen refreshed its databases daily—not only its culinary databases, but its legal ones, too."

"Excellent point, Number Seven!" said One, clapping its hands. "Well-reasoned, indeed. Number Five, doesn't the contradiction that Seven has described give you cause to change your vote?"

"It's not a contradiction," said Julio.

Number Eleven crossed its arms over its chest and tipped back its head to gaze at the virtual ceiling. "Here we go again."

"Why not?" said Number Seven.

"Euthanasia isn't legal here in the United States, but it is in Europe."

"Give it up," said Eleven.

"No, listen." Julio stood up in the cubicle and clenched his fists on the controls, inadvertently making his bot's arms spin. "Sorry, wait a minute." He secured the arms and went on. "The Ellises had the International Model. So the databases it checked—both culinary and legal—were European as well as American."

"That's interesting," said Seven. "But wouldn't the legal information it got from both sources be at cross-purposes?"

"Maybe," said Julio.

"Then why would it prioritize the European sources, rather than the American ones, given that the Ellises live here, not in Europe?" said Seven.

"Maybe the kitchen defaulted to the direction its owners were taking."

"How so?"

"Mrs. Ellis's friends said that she was 'cooking her way around the Mediterranean.' If she routinely put the kitchen in the International Mode for cooking, then the kitchen might have given priority to Europe's laws and cultural assumptions. Don't you see? That would follow from its generative matrix: to adapt itself to the habits and desires of its owners."

"But that's ridiculous," said Eleven. "Gen-K is an American Company."

"But that would explain why the kitchen would have overridden the fail-safes," mused Seven.

"Yes!" said Julio, "Exactly! I love you!"

"Excuse me?" said Seven.

"Uh—sorry, I didn't think the mic would pick that up."

"He's clearly a lunatic," said Eleven.

"We'll have no name-calling in this Deliberation Room," said One.

All of the bots started talking at once. Julio tried to jump up and stand behind Seven, but found that his bot's range of motion was limited to the fifth chair at the table. Only bot Number One could pace the room, and it did so to get everyone's attention.

"Quiet, please. Be quiet," said One. "Why didn't the defense prioritize this angle?"

"The defense tried to raise doubts about almost everything," said Julio. "Maybe the priorities got mixed up in how the vidstream was edited."

"All those jump cuts?" said Seven.

"Right. But the defense did review the data stream: the queries that the kitchen put to legal databases here and across the Atlantic," said Julio. "Isn't that enough to prove a 'reasonable doubt'?"

"I still don't believe that the designers would be so stupid," said One. "It's their job to foresee such problems."

"Exactly," said Seven. "And that's why the defense kept trying to show how complicated the kitchen's programming is: there were subgroups of engineers who contributed from all over Europe, many more than those from over here. Maybe the neural nets they designed overrode the constraints that the American engineers put on killing a client."

"On purpose?" asked Two.

"Not necessarily. Those experts kept saying that the more complex a system, the more unpredictable it is," said Seven.

"Or maybe the basic concept that the Euro-groups introduced into the kitchen's neural nets was different," said Julio.

"How so?" said One.

"Well, isn't it a matter of semantics? In Europe, 'to euthanize' isn't the same as 'to kill,'" said Julio.

"That's just cockamamie," interjected Number Eleven. "They mean the same thing: to end life unnaturally, which is a sin."

"Unless you decide to subject Mrs. Ellis to the death penalty?" asked Julio.

"Now I get it," said Eight, pointing at Julio. "I bet you're one of those wimps who opposes the death penalty."

"If he is," said Eleven, "then he must have lied about it. That was one of the first questions those lawyer bots asked during the selection process."

"Great," said Twelve. "Can we kick Number Five out and call in an alternate? C'mon, let's vote on it."

Julio bit his lip. He had, indeed, lied about his attitude toward the death penalty, because he wanted the free trip to Acapulco. But he couldn't admit it now. "No, wait. I'm open-minded about the death penalty."

"Liar," said Eleven.

"Hold on," said Number One. "Mrs. Ellis is the one on trial, not Number Five."

"Yes," said Seven, "Let's get back to the facts."

They argued for the rest of the afternoon and took another vote before they left. Julio felt vindicated when the tally materialized on the scorescreen: ten to two. He was certain that Number Seven had changed her vote.

"What do we do now?" asked Eight.

"Let's continue the discussion tomorrow," said One. "More of you may change your minds after a good night's sleep."

"Fat chance," said Eleven.

"How long do we have to do this?" asked Two.

"Until we agree," said One.

"But what if we don't agree?" asked Nine.

"Then we hang," said Eleven.

"Maybe we should all say we lied about the death penalty. I don't want to hang," said Two.

The bots laughed, except for Julio, who wasn't sure whether Two meant the remark as a joke.

"The term means that we couldn't reach agreement, so the trial has to be redone with a new jury," said One.

"In Acapulco?" asked Two.

"Or the Bahamas—the court has resort property there, too," said Eleven.

"I thought the Bahamas disappeared in the last hurricane?" said Three.

"The resort is on one of those storm-proof platforms," Eleven said. "In the hurricane repellant zone."

"Yeah," said Six, "I was disappointed to be assigned to an Acapulco jury. I had wanted to check out the waterproof sand on New Bimini."

"So why don't we just go ahead and hang," said Twelve. "It's clear we're going nowhere."

"No," said Number One. "Not yet. The instructions say that the jurors should do their utmost to come to an agreement, so we need, at least, to sleep on it."

Some of the bots grumbled, but no one refused.

"Tomorrow, then. Nine o'clock sharp," said One, and the VR screen went dead.

Julio was on time the next morning, after a night of little sleep. He dozed briefly, but flinched awake after he dreamt of Mrs. Ellis being hung by a posse of purple bots. Sleep eluded him until dawn, just before the alarm rang. Now, seated in the deliberation cubicle, he clutched the thermos of coffee that he had brought, hoping it would tide him through the morning.

After the VR screen flashed on, Number One called another vote. The "Not Guilty" faction had gained a new member.

"That would be me," volunteered Seven. "Mulling the testimony over last night, I had an epiphany. I remembered how the defense kept insisting that there should have been fail-safes. Whether Mrs.— or even Mr.—Ellis programmed that machine to kill, isn't the issue. Nor should we debate whether the kitchen made its own decision. Either way, Mr. Ellis shouldn't have died. The fault lies with the corporation."

"So who voted 'Not Guilty' yesterday?" asked Eight.

"I did," Number One confessed. "At the end of the day, I found myself agreeing with Number Five: there are just too many other possible explanations for Mr. Ellis's death. I think that those Euro-programmers may have set it all up. Doesn't anyone else agree, besides Five and Seven?"

But the other bots preferred the simple explanation: Mrs. Ellis was to blame. Number One insisted that they go around the table and explain the reasons for their votes. As the "Guilty" faction spoke, Julio marveled that each bot, while agreeing that Mrs. Ellis was a murderer, had a different explanation of her methods and motivations, many of which bore no resemblance to the evidence. Dispirited, he decided to let Number One and Number Seven expose the contradictions in the jurors' rationales. But none of the bots changed their views.

"Number Four," said One. "You're the last to speak. In fact, you haven't said anything at all during the whole deliberation process. Tell us, why did you vote 'guilty'?"

There was a long pause, and One repeated the question. After another pause, Number Four stirred. "Whoa—what was that? Fire?! Where's the exit?"

"I activated the wake up alarm in your cubicle, Four," One said and repeated the question a third time.

"Why is she guilty? That's easy. I can just tell."

"How can you tell?" Julio asked, speaking for the first time that morning. "You've got to have a reason."

"Of course I do," said Four. "My gut tells me she's guilty."

"But that's not a reason," Julio said.

"It's enough for me. I'm a great judge of human character," said the bot.

After the lunch break, the vote was unchanged. Number One forwarded the decision to the judge, who urged them to reconsider.

"She insists that we at least spend the afternoon trying to resolve our differences," said One.

Julio admired Number One for its effort over the next several hours, for by that time Number Seven had also backed away from trying to argue with the "Guilty" faction, who became increasingly belligerent. At 4:30, Number One gave up, too.

"May I at least appeal to you all as taxpayers? Consider the costs of sending another group of jurors to Acapulco," said One.

"Or New Bimini!" said Eleven.

"There's more of us who think she's guilty, so maybe you three should do the taxpayers a favor and change your minds," said Two.

After another appeal to reconsider, the Judge reluctantly accepted their decision. Julio thought that there would be some sort of formality for ending their service, but Number One said a curt "Thank you" and the screen went dead.

Julio tucked his thermos into his coat pocket and hopped onto the elevator, whose doors glided open for him as soon as he reached his floor's vestibule. But the car went up instead of down, all the way to the sixtieth floor.

During its descent, it stopped at almost every floor. As more and more people stepped aboard, Julio recognized a few jurors from the Ellis trial: the paunchy man, who wore a suit now, instead of a Hawaiian shirt, and the girl with the backpack. Everyone stood silently, facing forward and passively moving further back when a new person stepped on.

After floor forty-three, the car reached capacity. When the doors opened again at other floors, people declined to board because the car was so full. But at twenty-five, a woman held the car up.

"Let me on, I'm in a hurry."

"Sorry, Miss," said a man. "Can't you see there's no room?"

Stuck in the rear, Julio tried to peer over people's shoulders to catch a glimpse of her. All he saw was the peak of a stylish felt hat.

"That's no way to treat a lady," she said. "I guess I'll have to keep my hand on the door until one of you changes your mind."

Several passengers spoke up at once.

"We're all in a hurry."

"Yeah, we're dying for some fresh air."

"Who do you think you are?"

But Julio was sick of arguing. "Wait a minute, I'll get off. I'm suffocating back here anyway. I don't mind taking the stairs."

More people seemed annoyed by his chivalry than by the woman's demands, but they let him squeeze by. Coming up even with the doors, he found himself face-to-face with Iris, who gave him a magnanimous smile.

"Seven!" he said, trying to grab her iridescent hand. "Wait for me in the lobby—let's have a drink."

"C'mon buddy, you said you'd get off," a man behind him grumbled and gave him a sharp push between the shoulder blades. Julio stumbled out of the elevator. Unable to balance, he fell to one knee on the concrete floor.

Iris swept by him and took her place at the front of the car. She adjusted the shoulder straps on her enormous purse and unzipped her fur-trimmed jacket to reveal the slinky camisole beneath.

"Eleven," she called out, pulling back the jacket to expose her yellow juror badge. "Adios, kiddo."

Feeling as if he'd been punched, Julio leaped up and slammed his thumb against the call button. The doors froze. "No private penthouse elevator?" he whispered. "What a hardship."

She stabbed her finger on the inside button panel. "I've already complained about that—"

"What's the problem?" someone shouted from the back of the car.

"She's holding us up," said a woman beside Iris.

"Let me assist," said Julio, with icy politeness. He grabbed Iris by the wrist and pulled her into the vestibule. The elevator doors snicked shut.

She tore her wrist away and the rainbow colors blurred into dull blotches where his fingers had dug into the skin. "Look—you've ruined the lacquer!" she said, backing away from him.

"You call that a crisis?" said Julio, rocking back on his heels.

"That's property damage and assault. You have no idea how much even a touch-up will cost!"

"Give me a break. Swimming in the hotel pool, or sun-bathing didn't hurt your biometallic lacquer, but now it's ruined?"

"I used chlorine and UV resistant creams every time I left my room. And the Weather-All brand suffices here," she said. "Until now. I'll sue—and there are witnesses." She pointed to the surveillance camera.

"Witnesses to your narcissism?"

"Oh, and you think that you've been appointed judge now as well as jury?"

"Why not? At least I base my judgments on reason. Go ahead and sue me. The court will dismiss it as frivolous whining from a wealthy bitch."

Iris threw back her shoulders. "Get over yourself, kiddo. Here are the facts. I worked forty years as a college librarian in Milwaukee. When I retired, I moved to Chicago and spent half my life savings at Michelangelo's. I'm proud of this body, and the maintenance isn't cheap. You've sullied my investment."

Julio laughed. "You can afford the penthouse and limousine service in Acapulco, but can't afford maintenance on a designer body? Give me a break!"

"That's right, kiddo," she snapped. "The penthouse, the first class flight, the limousine are all beyond my means." She reversed her badge to display an engraved metal backing.

"But as a platinum member of the Frequent Jurors Program, I'm entitled to upgrades."

"What? I thought it was almost impossible to be chosen for Vacation Jury Duty—"

"Smoke and mirrors, kiddo. You fell for the marketing hype, just like with that kitchen. Here's the reality: there are spaces available to Frequent Jurors on every trial, even the Vacation stints. Didn't you read the service agreement?"

Julio felt his cheeks grow hot. "Who has time for that? After the lawyers selected me, I just clicked the 'I agree' box on the screen."

Iris smiled serenely. "As a former librarian, I recommend that you always make time for reading. In Acapulco, I spent my free time rereading *War and Peace*. Tell me, Number Five, did you discover the resort's fine collection of e-books? Or were you too busy ogling women?"

"That's not fair." Julio's voice rose. "You led me on—"

"Led you on? C'mon kiddo, the world doesn't revolve around you.

I aim to look beautiful wherever I go. And on my pension, I can afford to look great, and to travel as well, thanks to the Frequent Jurors Program." Iris raised her chin and tucked a few stray wisps of copper hair beneath her felt hat. "McConnery Ellis and her rich friends may have been luncheoning their way around the Mediterranean, but I intend to see it before I die."

She stabbed the call button again and glanced over her shoulder at Julio. "I've been short-listed for a Federal Grand Jury Cruise of Italy."

A second elevator arrived, almost as full as the previous one. People shuffled back to make enough space for both Julio and Iris. Iris hurried onto the car and set her purse down in the empty place beside her. The bell pinged.

"But before I go anywhere," she said as the doors began to close, "I'll be putting in a claim against you for reimbursement of the cost to fix my skin lacquer."

Julio stepped forward to stop the doors and then pulled back, clenching his coat in his hands.

"Thanks, but I'd rather take the stairs," he said to the empty vestibule.

He opened the fire door and sprinted down the twenty-five flights to the lobby, where he paused to watch the number display illuminate as Iris's car stopped at every floor. Waiting to have the court officials erase their surveillance software from his phone, he stood straight-backed, head held high, on the assumption that Iris stood somewhere in the line behind him. But after the clerk certified that his phone was clear, Julio shrugged on his coat and did not see Iris as he walked past the line on his way to the exit. He contented himself by assuming that, as a Frequent Juror, she had agreed to a permanent installation of court spyware on her phone.

Outside, snow flurries gusted, illuminated by the streetlights. Julio picked his way between drifts to the bus shelter. Switching on the shelter's heat lamps, he rebooted the phone and checked his sports stream for news of the Bulls, but the feed was interrupted by two triple star "ULTRA-URGENT" message alerts: one from Shea, "Call ASAP!!" the other from Toni, "Decision time." His stomach clenched.

In no mood for Toni, he called Shea first, certain she would still be at work after 5:00. Signing on, she yawned and rubbed her eyes, smearing her mascara. Her collar was wrinkled, and her power bob haircut uncharacteristically ragged. Julio was accustomed to her sour expression, but she looked even more unpleasant than usual—as if she were the one who had recently flown in on a red-eye.

He decided to cut her no slack. "What was the point of sending all those work orders? I told you I wouldn't have phone access in Acapulco."

"Sorry—I didn't generate those. Upper management mandated installation of a new system. The transition's been rocky." She gave him one of her rare smiles. "Only three days left. Screw management—you're lucky to be deliberating instead of here. But you should at least join us at Miller's for a beer on Friday."

"What's the occasion?"

"You didn't read the lay-off notice? Allied sent it the night before you left for Acapulco."

"But retaliation for jury service is illegal—"

"It's not retaliation. We're terminated. All of us.

Allied's been bought out by DelivRite. Hostile takeover. They're stripping us clean. That's why the system's messed up. They're replacing the remaining human claims reps with bots equipped with affect recognition technology."

Julio snorted. "DelivRite thinks it takes a bot to recognize that claims customers are angry?"

"I know." Shea's voice was tense. "But these bots will stay on script. And the script's being rewritten to absolve DelivRite of blame for crappy packaging."

Julio enjoyed hearing Shea swear. Suddenly, he felt sorry for her. "I finished deliberating this afternoon. Do you want me to come in and help?"

Shea smiled again. "No, don't worry about it. I won't tell the transition team you're free. Just be sure to stop by Miller's on Friday."

"Will do."

"DelivRite's probably given you the standard package—two weeks pay and an extra month of health insurance. Let me know if you need a reference."

"Thanks. See you Friday."

Julio signed off and stamped his feet to shake off the cold. He felt elated to be free of Allied, but terrified about whether he could afford to keep his micro apartment. He did not want to tell Toni about his situation. But he was curious about her last message. Had she beat him to the punch and decided to move on? He clicked the scrollbar icon.

She lounged on the couch in her apartment, her angular face softened by the phonecam's glow. "Are you back? Did you watch my last message?! I finaled in the Mile High Marathon on Saturday! Second prize: my choice of a complete make-over at Michelangelo's on Michigan Avenue, or a scuba cruise for two of the drowned cities in the Bahama Triangle. You know, the hurricane repellant zone?" She winced and shifted position. "So. I've decided on the make-over. Not for you, but for me." She reoriented the phone so that it showed her legs stretched out and bolstered by pillows. An ice-pack covered her left knee. "The DelivRite building's stairs did a number on me, and Michelangelo's agreed to substitute a knee replacement for the breast augmentation in the beauty sculpting package. But this will probably be my last marathon. I can't afford to upgrade to the athlete quality knee joint." She smiled and winced again. "Please. Call when you get back. I miss you."

Julio nearly dropped the phone in his hurry to press the call back button. He let the phone ring for more than a minute, but Toni did not pick up. He checked the date of her message— two days ago—

and panicked, imagining her lean body sculpted into regimented curves and her skin blemished by an iridescent glaze. He recorded a hasty message—"Toni, I love you. Please, choose the trip—"

She signed on as he was speaking. "Julio! Sorry. I couldn't pick up right away. Had to grab an ice pack. Hang on." She eased herself onto the couch.

"Stay away from Michelangelo's!"

"Why? I thought you'd like the make-over. You know I hate putting on make-up, and the package includes permanent eyeliner and eyebrow tattoos."

"No. I was wrong—you don't need make-up. Or a wardrobe change. Or body sculpting. Just be yourself."

"But my knee—"

"Won't your insurance cover knee replacement?"

"Yes, but Michelangelo's could straighten my nose."

"Don't. I love your nose."

"But we're breaking up, right? You won't be the one to look at it."

"No. Let's not break up. Choose the trip. We'll go the Bahamas. I want a real vacation. With you."

"Wait—you've just been to Acapulco. You insisted on the Jury trip because Allied didn't give you vacation time—"

"I've been laid off. Look, Toni let's move in together. Your apartment or mine, I don't care. I can use the rest of my savings to help pay for your knee replacement. Or we can sue DelivRite. A personal injury claim. Those bastards."

"Julio, slow down. Are you all right? Where are you, anyway?"

"Done with the trial. And on my way to your place—if you'll have me."

"Okay. I haven't made any decisions yet. About you or Michelangelo's. We need to talk this out in person."

Julio glanced at the shelter's vidscreen to see how long he would have to wait for the next bus. Thirty minutes. "Of course. Can I get anything for you? Extra ice?" He grinned. "Maybe some good tequila?"

"What?" Toni raised her eyebrows in mock horror. "You didn't bring a bottle back from Acapulco? If you want to talk me into choosing the Caribbean, maybe you should ply me with rum. My beverage port has plenty of mixers."

Julio laughed. "Sure. And I'll try to find some fresh limes, too." He pulled up his hood. "See you soon."

The snow flurries thickened to steady, wet flakes. Hoping to hail a cab, Julio stepped away from the shelter and peered down the block.

No cars approached, and the Deliberation Center had disappeared in a fury of white.

Retreating to the shelter, Julio shoved the phone into his pocket, doubtful that any ride service would arrive before the bus in this weather. On the vidscreen, the arrival time—increased to forty minutes—scrolled beneath advertisements showing smiling people in deckchairs beside a pool shaped like the state of Illinois.

The header flashed: "Vacation Jury Duty! It's Real! It's Different! It's the Law!"

Not caring whether the sidewalks were plowed, Julio turned into the wind and began walking the ten blocks north to the Loop, where he could catch an El to Toni's place.

ABOUT THE AUTHOR

A writer and artist dedicated to multiple genres, **Meg Pontecorvo** earned an MFA in Poetry Writing from Washington University in St. Louis and is a 2010 graduate of the Odyssey Writing Workshop. Meg has published a novelette, "Grounded," in *Asimov's*, and her artwork in collage and pen has been featured in experimental video performances in the Bay Area. A native of Philadelphia, she grew up in the Midwest and now shares a small apartment with her partner and cats in San Francisco, where she cooks in a tech-free kitchen.

WANT MORE SCIENCE FICTION?
TURN THE PAGE FOR A SNEAK PEAK
OF THE POLITICAL SATIRE SCIENCE FICTION NOVEL,
CAMPAIGN 2100: GAME OF SCORPIONS
BY LARRY HODGES

Thank you for reading!
We hope you'll leave an honest review at Amazon,
Goodreads, or wherever you discuss books online.

Leaving a review means a lot for the author and editors who
worked so hard to create this book.

Please sign up for our newsletter for news about upcoming
titles, submission opportunities, special discounts, & more.

WorldWeaverPress.com/newsletter-signup

Campaign 2100: Game of Scorpions
by Larry Hodges

CHAPTER ONE:
THE CHANGING OF THE SCORPIONS
Noon, Friday, January 20, 2096

What have I done?

The thought raced through Toby Platt's mind as he stood in the shadows of the Twin Towers in Lower Manhattan as the live orchestra played *Hail to the Chief.* He was sick of the song. He was sick of the cold, misty weather. Above all, he was sick of Corbin Dubois, the president-elect, the man he'd made the next president of Earth.

The music was in honor of President-for-five-more-minutes Jing Xu. The Chinese man stood at a lectern, side by side with Dubois. The two blue-suited mortal enemies smiled and waved at the huge crowd of dignitaries. Then Xu turned to Dubois, and they shook hands, one scorpion to another. Except, Toby thought, some are more scorpion than others.

All politicians are scorpions. Bruce, his former top aide, once said that a politician without a sting was like a ping-pong player without a paddle. And yet it was how—and why—they used that stinger that mattered. Xu had quite a sting, as they'd learned during the campaign. Xu the president wasn't so bad, but Xu the politician— well, you didn't get to be leader of the world without a little scorpion blood.

But Dubois just stung anyone who got in his way, often using Toby's own words. Whether it was hunger in Asia and Africa, Mormon-Israeli strife in Utah, or even piracy in the South China Sea, they were all just political points to the Dubois campaign. Toby had five more years of it to look forward to—five years of the never-ending campaign that all worldwide offices had become. He could feel the deadness in him growing.

Which was why Toby had decided to resign.

The plump Frenchman was Napoleonic short, a comparison they'd used with great success in the election. His bleached white hair twisted upward to a point, his sideburns splayed sideways, and his beard looked like a series of long, white icicles. With hair shooting in all directions like an exploding star, he was an easy caricature for the world's late night comics. Add the archaic red tie and the perpetually darting eyes, and Dubois had a memorable face that had grown on voters. So did his American cowboy persona, which every Frenchman publicly detested but privately wanted to emulate. The white hair made him look older than his 45 years.

It seemed wrong to Toby that this man would take the oath of office at the foot of the Twin Towers, with their storied histories. There was no sight more majestic, more inspirational than these monuments to human resilience. Twice they had been destroyed, and twice rebuilt, the second time at well over twice the height of the originals. Those two terrorist acts had marked the start and end of the Age of Terror. The second had led to world government, and to the likes of Dubois.

At three thousand feet, they were the tallest skyscrapers in the world and one of the Seven Wonders of the Modern World. They housed the World Congress; The North Tower the House of Representatives, the South Tower the World Senate. Nearly all the Representatives and Senators were in attendance for the inauguration.

Dubois stepped back from the lectern and stood next to Toby, a little apart from the other dignitaries. Xu began the customary farewell address, which was scheduled for a mercifully short five minutes.

"We're almost there," Dubois said, patting Toby on the back as they listened to Xu's gracious words.

"I'm resigning," Toby blurted out, his voice low enough so others would not hear.

Dubois turned and stared at him. Then he smiled. "No you're not." He went back to watching Xu.

"No, really," Toby said. "We haven't agreed on anything in years. I can't stay."

"We'll work it out," Dubois said without looking at him.

A dozen times Toby had decided to leave, a dozen times he'd decided to stay, to at least finish the campaign. Nobody runs a worldwide campaign and then quits on the verge of winning. They had won, and now he could walk away as a famously successful campaign director.

"We can't work it out," Toby said. "You can bring in anyone now, so you don't need me."

Dubois turned his piercing eyes back on him, the smile still frozen on his face. "You're my political guru. You got me here. I need you to handle the politics the next five years, and the next campaign. We're great together!"

Toby shook his head. "It's over. I resign, effective the instant you become president."

The smile was gone, replaced by the famous Dubois glare, something Toby had never faced before, though he'd seen many others wilt under it. "You do this, and you'll never work in politics again."

Toby knew that was coming. "I know."

"Neither will your daughter."

Toby froze. Lara and Bruce had been his top advisors. When Bruce left to return to the ping-pong circuit, Lara was the only life he really had outside politics. Which somehow seemed contradictory, since Lara's whole life was also politics. Of course, Toby had a wife and son as well, though he rarely saw them.

"You wouldn't—"

"Plug the mouth hole, and please don't say I wouldn't dare," Dubois said. "You know I would. Isn't that why you're resigning in the first place? And now, why you won't? So let's just forget we had this discussion."

"You can't—"

"You and Lara are the only advisors I trust," Dubois said. "We're going to do great things these next five years. We'll even go moderate, if that's what you want. You'll both be a part of it. Meet me in the Red Room in one hour so we can make plans. That's all."

It took more than a penetrating stare to force someone to submit. You had to have a weapon to back it up. Toby glanced over at Lara, who stood with the other dignitaries, a broad smile on her face on this triumphant day. Dubois had the stare and the weapon.

Ice cold anger rose in him, but what else was new? Once upon a time he would have acted on his anger. Now it was just another emotion to control. He'd become good at that.

Toby gave a short nod. Dubois nodded back. They went back to listening to Xu's speech, which was already over the allotted time. Security floaters flew in slow circles around the towers, guarding the airspace like hawks, ready to dive and attack if the unthinkable were to happen.

Just when Toby thought they were going to have to shoot him to get him off, Xu turned and took his seat off to the side, ceding the lectern to Dubois. The Chief Justice of the United States of Earth approached the lectern. Dubois raised his right hand, his left on a stack of religious scriptures—Christian and Jewish Bibles, the Muslim Quran, the Hindu Vedas, the Buddhist Buddhavacana, the Confucianism Analects, the Sikh Adi Granth, the Book of Mormon, and several others.

Toby wanted to run to the podium and yell *"Stop! A terrible mistake has been made!"* But he did not.

The Chief Justice spoke the words, and Dubois recited them back. *"I do solemnly swear that I will faithfully execute the office of President of the United States of Earth, and will to the best of my ability, preserve, protect, and defend the Constitution of the United States of Earth."*

The changing of the scorpions was complete. Toby adjusted the fading purple scarf he always wore, even in warm weather. It seemed entirely out of place. Long ago he'd pulled it off a dead victim of his past idealism.

"Isn't it great, Dad? *We did it!*" Lara's beaming smile contrasted with his own outlook. How many other families ran worldwide elections as their main father-daughter activity?

Lara's upbeat outlook, quick mind, and long, shiny black hair had earned her spot as campaign spokesperson, but she'd been much more than that. They both wore "Win with Corbin!" buttons, with a small Coca-Cola logo centered over the words.

Missing from the team was Bruce Sims, table tennis champion and Lara's almost fiancé, who'd abandoned the campaign months before. Toby wondered if Bruce was watching on his thought computer. Of course he was.

Dubois raised his arms over his head. When the crowd quieted, he lowered his arms and began to speak. Toby closed his eyes and mouthed the words he himself had written as Dubois spoke them. Inspiring words, promises and pledges. *Lots of sound and fury, signifying nothing*, he thought. *Who's the idiot here?*

The speech ended, the crowd cheered, and the orchestra leaped back into *Hail to the Chief* as Dubois began walking the VIP line, shaking hands. His bald and emaciated vice president followed, the always-frowning Rajan Persson, towering two feet over his boss.

Lara beamed at Toby. He forced a smile back. This was the culmination, the ultimate father-daughter moment, the reason why he'd stayed with Dubois, and would continue to do so. He didn't want to ruin it for her.

"We did it, Daddy!" she repeated, clenching her fists in the air. During the campaign, as his assistant, she'd made the final transition from daughter to woman in Toby's eyes, turning thirty in the process. He was only fifty, with rapidly balding reddish-brown hair that only bad genetics or a political campaign can give you. Lara gave his scarf a yank. "Just this once, could you take that smelly thing off?"

We did it, Daddy. The words wouldn't leave his mind as he fingered the scarf, watching Dubois shake hands and wave to his admirers. What would Vinny have said if he were here, alive, instead of just his scarf? Toby yanked the scarf off and jammed it in a pocket. He didn't deserve to wear it.

What have I done?

He stared off into space for a moment.

What can I do to fix this?

The answer was nothing. Not for five more years.

Who's worse, a bad king or the kingmaker?

CHAPTER TWO:
THE ARRIVAL
Tuesday, July 27, 2100

The spaceship landed shortly after 9:00 A.M. in front of the United Nations Building in East Manhattan, exactly four weeks before the start of the worldwide election for president.

The large black sphere, 20 feet in diameter, had plummeted out of the sky at a meteor's speed, then slowed in seconds until it came to a stop, floating five feet above the ground. No Earth vehicle could match that performance. There was no visible means of levitation underneath the ship, just a smooth, black surface. In most places on Earth there would have been panic. However, this was New York City, Earth's capital, where "alien" was just a matter of degree.

Crowds gathered, many broadcasting the images worldwide with their thought computers. A child threw a veggie dog against the black sphere, leaving dripping mustard on its side. Several other children dashed under the black sphere until stern parents pulled them back.

Within minutes, delegations of police arrived. They cordoned off the area around the black sphere to hold the crowds back, then sauntered about, not sure what to do about this strange ship that had fallen in their midst.

The chief of police stepped past the cordoning. There was no obvious door on the ship, whose shiny black surface was marred only by the dripping mustard. He rapped on the ship with his stick. "Anyone there?"

* * *

While the alien ship was landing, Toby and his daughter were in the Red Room in the United Nations Building—*The Bubble*—going over campaign strategies with the president and vice president.

On the wall to the left and right of the president's huge walnut desk were portraits of past world presidents, brightly lit from a chandelier and the sunlight through the windows. Interactive holomaps floated near the front wall. Lettered in blue on the soft red carpeting were the letters "POTUSE": *President of the United States of Earth.*

It hadn't always been the Red Room. When Wallace had been elected the world's first president in 2050, he'd painted the office green, to represent the environmental work needed to clean up after the nuclear wars of 2045. When Abrams succeeded him ten years later, he painted the room red, the color of the Conservative Party. Since that time the room had changed color and name whenever it changed parties. During the liberal Xu administration, it had been the Blue Room. Now it was the Red Room once again.

"We need to find a compromise," Toby said as he rose to his feet. "If we take either side, we lose the votes and funding from the other side." He fingered the fading purple scarf under his short beard. He'd lost weight this past year, and his green suit sagged loosely along the sides.

"You're going soft," said Lara. She walked over to the holomaps by the front wall, stopping in front of a shimmering map of North America. Colored dots indicated various voting regions, Conservative headquarters for each state, upcoming political events, and other data. "A compromise means you lose both sides," she said as she tapped her finger over two almost overlapping orange dots on purple Utah. One was Salt Lake City; the other New Israel. "Forget the Israelis, we need the Mormon vote. Get them angry, and you lose the Midwest and

Mexico." She waved her hand over the indicated regions. "Side with the Mormons, and you win all this."

"But we've always supported New Israel," President Dubois mumbled. He was seated at his desk, his mouth full of natural peanuts he was stuffing in a handful at a time, ignoring the bowl of artificial no-cal peanuts also on his desk. He'd gained thirty pounds the past four years, and was on his sixth set of blue suits as he moved up in waist size. "If the media starts calling me a hypocrite again I'll lose votes. They can do that all they want *after* the election."

A fly buzzing in the window behind Dubois brought Toby's attention away from the pungent peanut aroma. How had a fly made it past the best security system in the world? Toby watched it fly up and down against the window. Maybe it liked peanuts.

"We have to do something about the Salt Lake riots," Lara said, "and a crackdown on the Israelis solves the problem." As she looked side to side, her black pyramidal hair, reaching a point a foot over her head, stayed rigidly in place. The four corners looked sharp enough to use as a weapon. The new style was cultivated for the press and voters, but Toby hated the latest trend toward polyhedral hair.

Persson, the towering vice president, slouched in his chair, frowning in his baggy brown suit and black bolo tie. If he stood, his head would hit the chandelier, and his chin would be above everyone's head. "Sir, don't you think—"

"Plug the mouth hole, Rajan," the president snapped, pronouncing it with an exaggerated "Ray-Jan." He didn't bother to glance at his vice president, whose frown grew deeper. "I don't want to deal with the New Israel Lobby before the election. If you can keep them out of my face until then, I'm fine with whatever helps us best."

"Corbin," Toby said, pulling his attention away from the fly. "If you take sides in this, you *will* look like a hypocrite, and everyone will see that." There's a limit on how much we can hide you from the voters, he thought.

"Everyone?" Lara asked. "Aren't you the one who preaches that all politics is local, that nobody notices what politicians do until they're in their own back yard?"

"It's all local," Toby replied, "until they find out what you've been telling others."

"They rarely pay attention and find out, do they?" Lara turned back to the holomap, and jabbed her finger in the middle, somewhere in Kansas, her finger going through it like a gigantic missile. "Dad, North America is seven percent Jewish and fifteen percent Mormon. It has 88 electoral votes, 62 from the U.S., and the momentum as the second continental election in the world, and the first major one. If we let Ajala take North America and its electoral votes, the next thing we know he'll be moving in here and the place will be crawling with liberals. As campaign director, what do you *really* recommend?"

Crawling with liberals, Toby thought, watching the buzzing fly. He'd had his greatest successes running moderate conservative campaigns, which was why he was blackballed by the Liberal Party. Dubois had promised Toby that he'd lead as a moderate, but once in office, he'd gone back to his conservative roots. Toby had once considered himself a liberal, but he no longer was sure. Conservatives, liberals—there weren't any other options in a world dominated by the Conservative and Liberal Parties.

"Well?" Lara asked, bringing Toby out of his reverie.

"Don't forget about the New Israel Lobby and their funding," Toby said. "We need NIL." The fly's buzzing was irritating; couldn't housekeeping or security or *someone* take care of it? With all their guns and other weapons, wouldn't they have a flyswatter packed away somewhere?

"Shouldn't we at least—" Rajan began.

"Plug it," Dubois said. "Toby, how much of our money have we gotten from NIL?"

Toby pulled his attention away from the distraction at the window. "About ten percent. But if we turn our backs on them, they'll let us know very loudly. Besides, the Israelis aren't the ones who started the rioting, it was—"

"How much do we expect to get from them before the North American election next month?" Dubois asked.

"We've received—" Toby began.

"—nearly all we're going to get from them," Dubois finished for him.

"Meaning," Lara said, "we already have the NIL money and can still get the Mormon vote, if we play this right. If we emphasize low taxes and law and order, we'll keep the conservative vote. They won't even notice what's happening in Utah, except the law and order part. As you always say, Dad, throw some spiced vegetables to energize the base."

Toby shook his head. "It just isn't—"

"I think we have to go with Lara's plan," Dubois said. "Just before the election, I'll condemn the Israelis and side with the Mormons. The Israelis will have to give up the disputed areas."

Toby knew he'd lost another argument. He was arguing with his heart instead of his head. He knew the saying: liberals have no head, conservatives no heart. Where did he fit in?

They'd been through a long primary campaign, but they'd easily won the Conservative nomination at the convention. Soon he'd have to make some tough "the end justifies the means" decisions in the upcoming general election. He remembered long ago having great difficulty with such decisions. Then he'd been introduced to the drug Eth, which took away moral constraints. It solved the problem, as long as he didn't get caught taking the illegal drug. It wasn't a magic bullet; you still had to choose to take the drug, knowing its effects, which was a moral dilemma in itself. This meeting would have been a lot easier for him if he'd taken some in advance. Fortunately—or perhaps unfortunately—he'd quit the habit after the 2095 election. It had been his decision to take Eth back then, and the consequences were his alone.

He couldn't argue with the hard political facts, since he was supposedly in charge of them. *Politics*, he thought. Once it had inspired him. "Poli" meant many, "tic" meant bloodsucker, so "politics" was just "many bloodsuckers." He was one of them.

As the glorified Campaign Director, he had about as much influence on the issues as the buzzing fly on the wall.

And once again, he knew, Israel was doomed. The establishment of New Israel outside Salt Lake City fifty years before had led to nothing but conflict. They'd won many votes in the last election by promising to resolve the ongoing Israeli-Mormon conflict; now, just before the next election, they were going to do so. Israel had once been destroyed by nuclear bombs; now it would be destroyed again, this time by administrative fiat.

Damn fly! Maybe he couldn't save New Israel, but the fly had to go. He looked about for something to swat it with, and grabbed a paper document from Dubois's desk. It seemed archaic to use so much paper in this age of thought computers, like counting on one's fingers, but Dubois was old-fashioned in that regard—and paper would always be a staple in any type of office, no matter how many predicted its demise. And they did make handy anti-fly weapons. Toby glanced at the title: *North American Tree Repopulation Study: The Regreening of America.* As if that had a chance. He'd make better use of it.

"Excuse me a moment," he said, rolling the paper into a cylinder. Then he realized that Dubois, Lara, and Persson were looking off into space, their eyes vacant. The words *"Breaking News!"* appeared in the air in front of him, and he now heard the words in his mind, care of his thought computer.

"TC on," he said under his breath, and the World News Network broadcast screen appeared before him. No one else could see or hear it, just as he couldn't see or hear the broadcasts the others were watching. The thought computers, implanted in their heads, played directly into the optical and auditory portions of their brains.

The WNN showed pictures surrounding what was apparently an

alien ship. A disembodied women's head on the lower right gave all the information available—essentially nothing. A scientist came on and explained how nothing on Earth could come out of the sky at such a speed, and how the alien could be a threat. Then the woman's head returned.

Toby stared at the black ship. Was this a prank, or could it actually be an alien, an actual first contact? His heart was racing. He realized he'd crushed the anti-fly weapon in his hand. He tossed it aside. Maybe the aliens could swat humanity like he could swat a fly. But a single ship that could probably fit in the Red Room didn't seem like an armada out to destroy humanity. He took a deep breath. First contact. On our watch.

"TC off," he whispered when the report degenerated to repeating itself, and found the president and Lara already in animated discussion. The fly now stood directly in front of Dubois on his desk, seeming to stare at Toby. Then it flew back to the window and continued its irritating buzzing.

Four aides came through the door at a run, all talking at once. They surrounded the president like bees around a beehive.

Dubois slammed his fist on his desk. "Shut up, all of you!" He pointed at each of the aides in turn. "You, you, you, and you, get out!" After a few seconds of blanching, the aides left, also at a near run.

"The last thing we need right now," Dubois said, "are a bunch of self-important lowbodies who think they know everything but know nothing of the political implications of anything. Who knows what's really going on with that ship, and how it'll affect the election?"

Like a laser beam fixed on a target, Toby thought, Dubois had zeroed in on the political aspect. Toby knew he'd once been like that, but not in recent years. At least he didn't think so.

"It could be an attack," Lara said. "Call out the guard, and if anything from that thing so much as sticks out its tongue, blast it. Of course, it might be a hoax."

"Why," Toby asked, "would you even consider attacking when this supposedly alien ship has done nothing hostile?"

Lara gave her most ingratiating smile. "Strong and wrong beat meek and weak. You said that, remember?"

Persson still sat on the couch, looking down at the president, who paced back and forth. "Perhaps we should—"

"Plug it." The president came to a stop. "If I go out there and play the 'welcoming leader' role, and it's some prank or something, I'll look like a fool."

"This is no hoax," Toby said. "There's nothing like that in the USE air force, or any other regional air force."

"How do you know?" Lara asked. "That's what they said about black helicopters."

"You think we have black spheres in the air force that can move like that thing did?"

Lara began to protest, but Dubois silenced her with a raised hand. "If these are real aliens, then I'm the one who's going to welcome them to Earth and get the credit. If we play this right, I can ride this to victory."

Persson began to say something, but changed his mind at a glance from the president.

"Sir," Toby said, "this could be the biggest thing this century—"

"All seven months of it," Lara interrupted. "Unless you're one of those potato-heads from the university who say the century doesn't start till next January."

"—and I believe we need to put politics aside for now and just see how this goes."

"Why would we do that?" Lara asked. "Heck, we can play this either way. Corbin can act all presidential, welcoming foreign dignitaries to Earth, or he can turn on the 'get tough on aliens' shtick, just like he did with the African émigrés last year. We win either way."

"And if it's a hoax?" Dubois asked.

"Then," Lara said, "you get to play the 'law and order' role when you deal with those idiots. It's win-win."

The president nodded. "Rajan, call the Army Chief to set up security. Toby, Lara, I'm going to need a welcoming speech. This is going to be historic, and people will read my words for centuries. And this could win the election. Get cracking."

On the way out, Toby alerted maintenance about the fly.

***

CAMPAIGN 2100: GAME OF SCORPIONS
by Larry Hodges
Earth's two-party politics is about to get an alien interloper.

Available now in paperback or ebook from World Weaver Press.

MORE SCIENCE FICTION
FROM WORLD WEAVER PRESS

FAR ORBIT: SPECULATIVE SPACE ADVENTURES
Science fiction in the Grand Tradition—Anthology
Edited by Bascomb James

Smart, engaging stories that take us back to a time when science fiction was fun and informative, pithy and piquant—when speculative fiction transported us from the everyday grind and left us wondrously satisfied. Showcasing the breadth of Grand Tradition stories, from 1940s-style pulp to realistic hard SF, from noir and horror SF to spaceships, alien uplift, and action-adventure motifs, Far Orbit's diversity of Grand Tradition stories makes it easy for every SF fan to find a favorite.

FAR ORBIT APOGEE
Modern space adventures—Anthology
Edited by Bascomb James

Far Orbit Apogee takes all of the fun-to-read adventure, ingenuity, and heroism of mid-century pulp fiction and reshapes it into modern space adventures crafted by a new generation of writers. Follow the adventures of heroic scientists, lunar detectives, space dragons, robots, interstellar pirates, gun slingers, and other memorable and diverse characters as they wrestle with adversity beyond the borders of our small blue marble.

Featuring stories from Jennnifer Campbell-Hicks, Dave Creek, Eric Del Carlo, Dominic Dulley, Nestor Delfino, Milo James Fowler, Julie Frost, Sam S. Kepfield, Keven R. Pittsinger, Wendy Sparrow, Anna Salonen, James Van Pelt, and Jay Werkheiser.

BITE SOMEBODY
by Sara Dobie Bauer

"Do you want to be perfect?"

That's what Danny asked Celia the night he turned her into a vampire. Three months have passed since, and immortality didn't transform her into the glamorous, sexy vamp she was expecting, but left her awkward, lonely, and working at a Florida gas station. On top of that, she's a giant screw-up of an immortal, because the only blood she consumes is from illegally obtained hospital blood bags.

What she needs to do—according to her moody vampire friend Imogene—is just ... *bite somebody.* But Celia wants her first bite to be special, and she has yet to meet Mr. Right Bite. Then, Ian moves in next door. His scent creeps through her kitchen wall and makes her nose tingle, but insecure Celia can't bring herself to meet the guy face-to-face.

When she finally gets a look at Ian's cyclist physique, curly black hair, and sun-kissed skin, other parts of Celia tingle, as well. Could he be the first bite she's been waiting for to complete her vampire transformation? His kisses certainly have a way of making her fangs throb.

Just when Celia starts to believe Ian may be the fairy tale ending she always wanted, her jerk of a creator returns to town, which spells nothing but trouble for everyone involved.

OPAL

by Kristina Wojtaszek

White as snow, stained with blood, her talons black as ebony...

In this retwisting of the classic Snow White tale, the daughter of an owl is forced into human shape by a wizard who's come to guide her from her wintry tundra home down to the colorful world of men and Fae, and the father she's never known. She struggles with her human shape and grieves for her dead mother—a mother whose past she must unravel if men and Fae are to live peacefully together.

Trapped in a Fae-made spell, Androw waits for the one who can free him. A boy raised to be king, he sought refuge from his abusive father in the Fae tales his mother spun. When it was too much to bear, he ran away, dragging his anger and guilt with him, pursuing shadowy trails deep within the Dark Woods of the Fae, seeking the truth in tales, and salvation in the eyes of a snowy hare. But many years have passed since the snowy hare turned to woman and the woman winged away on the winds of a winter storm leaving Androw prisoner behind walls of his own making—a prison that will hold him forever unless the daughter of an owl can save him.

CHAR

by Kristina Wojtaszek

Fire is never tame—least of all the flames of our own kindling.

Raised in isolation by the secretive Circle of Seven, Luna is one of the few powerful beings left in a world dominated by man. Versed in ancient fairy tales and the language of plants, Luna struggles to control her powers over fire. When her mentor dies in Luna's arms, she is forced into a centuries-long struggle against the gravest enemy of all Fae-kind—the very enemy that left her orphaned. In order to save her people, Luna must rewrite their history by entering a door in the mountain and passing back through time. But when the lives of those she loves come under threat, her rage destroys a forest, and everything in it. Now called The Char Witch, she is cursed to live alone, her name and the name of her people forgotten.

Until she hears a knock upon her long-sealed door.

FAE

An Anthology of Fairies
edited by Rhonda Parrish

Meet Robin Goodfellow as you've never seen him before, watch damsels in distress rescue themselves, get swept away with the selkies and enjoy tales of hobs, green men, pixies and phookas. One thing is for certain, these are not your grandmother's fairy tales.

Fairies have been both mischievous and malignant creatures throughout history. They've dwelt in forests, collected teeth or crafted shoes. Fae is full of stories that honor that rich history while exploring new and interesting takes on the fair folk from castles to computer technologies and modern midwifing, the Old World to Indianapolis.

With an introduction by Sara Cleto and Brittany Warman, and all new stories from Sidney Blaylock Jr., Amanda Block, Kari Castor, Beth Cato, Liz Colter, Rhonda Eikamp, Lor Graham, Alexis A. Hunter, L.S. Johnson, Jon Arthur Kitson, Adria Laycraft, Lauren Liebowitz, Christine Morgan, Shannon Phillips, Sara Puls, Laura VanArendonk Baugh, and Kristina Wojtaszek.

CORVIDAE
Rhonda Parrish's Magical Menageries, Volume Two

SCARECROW
Rhonda Parrish's Magical Menageries, Volume Three

SIRENS
Rhonda Parrish's Magical Menageries, Volume Four

EQUUS
Rhonda Parrish's Magical Menageries, Volume Five

FALLING OF THE MOON
MOONFALL MAYHEM, BOOK ONE
A.E. DECKER

If Ascot wants a Happy Ending, she'll have to write it herself!

In the gloomy mountains of Shadowvale, Ascot Abberdorf is expected to marry a lugubrious Count and settle down to a quiet life terrorizing the villagers. Instead, armed with a book of fairy tales, her faithful bat-winged cat, and whatever silverware she can pinch, Ascot heads east, to the mysterious Daylands, where her book promises she can find True Love and Happily Ever After, if she only follows her heart.

Watch for MOONFALL MAYHEM: Book Two, forthcoming from World Weaver Press in Fall 2016!

For more on these and other titles

visit WorldWeaverPress.com

* * *

World Weaver Press, LLC

Publishing fantasy, paranormal, and science fiction.

We believe in great storytelling.

worldweaverpress.com

Made in the USA
Middletown, DE
10 July 2016